# THE MARATHON OF SHADOWS

R.R. MARTINEZ

iUniverse, Inc.
New York  Bloomington

iUniverse books may be ordered through booksellers or by contacting:

iUniverse
1663 Liberty Drive
Bloomington, IN 47403
www.iuniverse.com
1-800-Authors (1-800-288-4677)

Because of the dynamic nature of the Internet, any Web addresses or links contained in this book
may have changed since publication and may no longer be valid. The views expressed in this work
are solely those of the author and do not necessarily reflect the views of the publisher, and the publisher
hereby disclaims any responsibility for them.

ISBN: 978-1-4502-2230-3 (sc)
ISBN: 978-1-4502-2231-0 (ebook)

Printed in the United States of America

iUniverse rev. date: 05/06/2010

> They say time changes things, but actually
> you have to change them yourself.

*Andy Warhol*

In the year 2040 the ability to genetically alter your child before birth is common. The. technology was developed by two married scientist in Brussels, they were both Aryan supremacist who wanted their children to be vastly superior to the endless stream of Arabic children who were coming into Flanders. Their experiments worked and both children, Jan and Piet, had higher IQ's than Edward Lorenz. However, as teenagers they came to a conclusion that even with their intellect there wasn't anything they could make that wouldn't be eventually warped and used for evil, so they killed themselves, the parents despondent also killed themselves. The books and all their work was sold by the landlord to his cousin, who seeing that it was over his head put it up for auction and was bought by the Al-ASHA development corp. of Saudi Arabia.

They were able to duplicate the work and also made many modifications including one for mood, since as IQ increased so did the possibility of severe depression. Once the work was completed, they sold it to the UN for an undisclosed amount. The UN made it available first to under developed countries then to the developed countries for a much higher price. This produced smarter stronger and more attractive babies every generation, greatly improving the living conditions of the under developed countries which got the technology for free and created a super ruling class. The only group to really lose out was the middle class in developed countries who if they couldn't afford the huge fees that the UN charged or where not willing to take on another mortgage to pay for it, got to see even their brightest kid's fall behind as their above average children were put into classes with genius from around the world.

This was especially true in the USA, where the wide use of genetic technology throughout the world coincided with the creation of the Christian Republican Party. This political party, which combined the southern evangelicals, the Spanish Opus Dei and the Chinese Christians regulated the democrats and republicans (now called the first Republican Party) to minor status. The CRP had managed to gain control of the house, senate and the presidency, additionally while being in power for 14 years they had managed to replace most of the machinery of government, the clerks, with their own operatives. The CRP outlawed genetic engineering along with a lot of other parts of American society that it felt was against god.

However, members of the CRP and all the parties along with the rich, purchased all applied genetics for themselves (discreetly) thereby ensuring their continued success. This also secured their ability to compete with their equally superior world counterparts, the middle and lower classes could not. Within two generations the middle class started to feel the pressures and tried to adapt. It started out with some parents enrolling their kids in advanced private schools during summer vacation, and then there was the "offload" learning craze. Which was simply a push to have more information at the child's disposal, each child was implanted with a little device that would connect them to the Internet and display all into their optic nerve, allowing access vast stores of public and private databases. Many had additional chips implanted in their brains, to offload computational and higher level logical problems. This worked for awhile but as the chips where readily available to all, some of the genetically altered revived them also, even if they really didn't need them.

As time passed life became more and more complicated since the ruling elite and the rest of the worlds IQ was moving ever upward they naturally created technologies and methodologies more suited to their own kind. Many in the US started to fall behind and the federal government stepped in. First, as is always the case with all governments, with those less likely to defend themselves. They started out with that section of society that has the lowest IQ and where having the hardest time surviving in an increasing technological environment. They offered them a fully paid upper middle class style with the understanding and medical assurances that they would not produce offspring. The thinking here of course was that you would eliminate the bottom and over time raise the "unworkable" IQ level subtly pushing all IQ's up.

However, September of 2III a brigade of ex Mexican army backed by some drug cartel's made a push to take over California from Los Angeles South to Mexico.This brigade was made up of about 5,500 with some mechanized support, with the addition of the cartel Special Forces added another 2000 men. Hardly a force to take attack the USA. However this war, which became known as the helix war went on for 6 months. The Americans discovering that while it's populace was busy infusing there children with the genetic enchantments that would help them to make a better life for themselves. Some drug cartels and military where enhancing children for their future military requirements.

This group of 7,500 men where hard to kill, as strong as five men, fast and each with the mind of Gingus khan and the body of the Spartans. Additionally since they had planned out there attack for quite some time they introduced weapons and techniques that the Americans had never seen and had a hard time with. Like dropping genetically altered flesh eating cockroaches on them. No one survived that drop and the area had to have 20 MOABS dropped on it just make sure none of the roaches survived. Even with American generals being more than a match for this group mentally, since they shared the same test tube, the solider on the field was vastly outmatch.

The group, which called itself La Neva Rasa, pushed it's way into LA in three months, killing hundreds of thousands along the way. The American generals planed and planed a counter attack. Pulling all there resources from all over the world for a big push. Which all agreed would finally win the day in about two years if they could hold them there until all was ready.

At this point a Sergeant Carlos Crispin of the Marines stepped in with a suggestion. Since most of the civilian population had either been killed or fled and those that were still there surly weren't as important as the entire country. Why don't we just pull our solider out and carpet bomb everything from LA down until everything is dead and destroyed. We wouldn't even have to use nukes since we could just as well release whatever biological agents we wanted to in our own country. The ruling class hadn't thought of this for the simple fact that as your IQ increases you simply value life more. In this case the original 16 million people had been brought down to some 6 million. Even the mass murders that the LNR committed were for purely tactical reasons and done in a way that the civilians would not suffer. 3 star general Chad Cary , who also was a concert pianist, put Carlos in charge of it and after three months of saturation bombing the war was over. Southern California was destroyed and the border to Mexico closed with orders to shoot on site anyone that tried to cross either way. American would recover, rebuild maybe but it didn't change the fact of what happened. The American generals and the federal government could see the writing on the wall and knew they had to do something. The people had to deal with a world were anything could be created in a local lab, they weren't ready for it.

Some people claim marriage interferes with romance, there's no doubt about it. Anytime you have romance, your wife is sure to interfere.

*Grocho Marx*

The University Park country club park in Bradenton Florida is the type of complex that used to bring retires down to Florida. A high end retirement community with its own golf course and three restaurants. All placed within walking distance to supermarkets and of course liquor stores, this one was known as the "Park" . Now it's home, like most of Florida, to the Omega generation. Retires that were still alive when someone made it profitable for people to live until they ran out of money. So you see individuals who are 100's of years old, running, playing tennis and fucking, the omega group has the highest concentration of SDT's's of any demographic. They looked just like people in there twenties did in the 1980's, but in their eyes you could almost see the crushing debt they had to put themselves under to look that way. And the smell, apparently no amount of scientific cocktail can get rid of that old person smell.

The Park came on some hard finical times after the war as most of the county did. The members of the board decided to open up some of the restaurants for wedding receptions to the locals to make some extra money. I was pacing in front of the lakeside, which really should now be called the mud pond or the mosquito incubator, since the lake without had seen better days. The tastefully built old style Florida hacienda room, which has enough room to cater a wedding for 220 and still have a nice hardwood dance floor, still looked elegant after all these years. That was the way of the world now, when you can live and live and live, motivation is the problem.

I was pacing and enjoying the only thing I liked about Florida, the Cohiba cigars, taking slow drags, trying to stall the walk back into the reception hall. It wasn't because of my newlywed wife, Pam, truly I couldn't remember loving anyone or anything in this world more than her. Yet sometimes when someone would ask me why I loved her, I would just say "cause", and I really meant it. No the stalling was caused by a huge case of buyers remorse that I was feeling. At the reception I finally got a chance to see her side and my side of the isles and the people in them.

I was born and raised in the Bronx my father had left the when he I young, just stayed long enough to pay for the DNA modifications my mother wanted, so my mother kept me pretty close. I had books as friends and became a computer geek and working for one of brokerage houses on Wall Street. I was an interesting job, with the each house looking for anyway to get a picoseconds edge on the competition. So my side of the isle was full beginning traders, computer geeks and administrators. While I noticed that Pam side of the isle seemed to be her girlfriends who are all on some mind altering drug.. with enough tattoos to fill most prisons I had seen cleaner woman in strip bars on the upper east side of New York..

My cigar is just about done when I see Bob, my new brother in law stumbling to me. Bob always stumbled, he was always drunk, high, something, always. Every child born in the last 100 years had every known addictive gene removed. But you have to give us humans credit, like a never ending space race every generation found something else to get addicted to, something the screening process had missed. There was a whole industry dedicated to figuring out what to sell us to ruin our lives. I tried to stall this moment, tried to wiggle out of it, but here it was. The moment Bob wanted to bond with me, all I could think of was, does he ever get a haircut.

"So Victor, bro, what are doing out here, want a beer?" Want a beer, this was it, the moment, made no less painful by the fact that whatever he was holding in his has couldn't really be called beer anymore.

"Not really, I not crazy about Beer."

"Oh, well you know it's an open bar and my sister is looking for you."

"Thanks" Of course I know it's an open bar, I'm paying for it, must remember to keep smiling.

"So Bob, let's just get this over with, you don't like me, I don't like you. We are never going to make that by the lake house, in wrangler jeans, sharing a beer and talking about the game commercial."

"Yeah.."

He took another drink of his beer and I took another drag of my cigar and just stood there for awhile.

"What I can tell you is I love your sister, and I'm always going to love your sister."

There she was, walking down the ramp, she looked like an angel floating down the handicapped ramp, maybe it was because I couldn't see her feet in that dress. I had done my required trawling for wanna be super-models in Ibiza, Brazil and the Hamptons. I had seen my share of enhanced pleasure creations in NYC, but she still made me look. The almond eyes from a Spain, small full lips and strawberry blond hair, which floated around her head. All on top of a body, that was some evil scientist sex goddess experiment, a little tits, a little ass and lot and lots of grace, mixed just right. Everyone said we where to young to get married, she was only 50 and me 55 and my friends made fun of me because she looked like a straight pleasure model, made to be some Arab sheiks play thing, I knew there was something else to her and we felt ready.

"Hummm this does not look warm and fuzzy."

Pam I guess like most woman could always tell what the emotional temperature and color was at any given moment.

"I was telling your brother how much I love you."

:"Ahhh but how do you feel about Bob?"

"He's not my type, ass to big"

We all laughed at this and went back in to the reception.

It was like a million receptions since the beginning of time, a father cried, a mother danced with a new son someone put a tie over their heads. Two people the single table made love in the closet, no one even knew them. The only part that really stood out for me was the dance with my new wife, the first dance ever with my wife. The party slowly winded, down one person here, one person there until there was only me.

Me and my check book and the caterer, florist, reception hall manager, limo drivers, band, until I get a small cramp in my hand from writing checks.. I walked outside and my brother Joe who is my best man is waiting for me.

"So you been married for almost a 7 hours, how is it so far?"

"Expensive."

"Don't worry I hear eventually you get to like the empty pockets. Anyway, this may be the only time you wife will be totally into to having sex with you so I think you need to go into that limo."

"Yeah, listen Joe; I paid for all the limos for the whole night, so go have fun with your little girl friend. By the way, were did you meet her?"

"I don't remember." With that he jumped into the limo and grabs his little friend in with him. Joe is my younger brother, real brother to, same sperm, and eggs frozen and unfrozen and genitally altered by the same team. We are probably closer then anyone else on this planet.

I walked across the street back to the hotel and went up to the maid of honor room. Julie was Pam's best friend in high school and for years after that.. They hadn't talked much in a while but when Pam called for her to be maid of honor, she said yes. Julie was stunning; a polish woman 5'9 with piercing blue eyes blond hair and a full body, but it was her venerability that got you. Her new husband Ben was an alcoholic the only reason he came to the wedding was the open bar and the only reason he was still in the room was the mini bar. . There really are few things in the world more powerfully magnetic then a beautiful woman who is lonely.

As soon as I opened the door I could tell Pam was drunk which pissed me off, I mean she couldn't keep it in check for one day.. Pam is an Irish drunk, or prone to fights and arguments, which didn't make for a great wedding night. On top of that, the glassy eyes, the same one her brother almost always had, meant it was going to be a long nigh and not in a good way I, sat on the couch with Julie while Pam and Ben drank and drank and drank.

"So Victor, we are now officially in the same club."

"What club is that?"

"The spouses of alcoholic's club, we should have a motto."

"How about, the keepers of the coffee pot?" which is what I wanted to put on right now.

"Hummm, how about when the cat's passed out the mice can play."

Julie smiled and paused for a minute and I could see her nipples getting hard and she smiled more to let him know I could look I decided to change the subject before something on me started getting hard "How about the cleaning of vomit club.."

"To morose, I was thinking those that never sleep."

"Or yeah that's a lot cheerier, why not the undead or Nosferatu"

That's when we heard the crash we rushed into the bland mass produced kitchen that is installed in everyone of these long term, sales men home from home hotel rooms to find Pam face first on the floor, knocked out. Having an alcoholic spouse is a lot like having an infant, eventually you can understand what they are saying even when no one else can. Julie found out that Ben and Pam where doing head stands on the kitchen counters while the other one was feeding them tequila. Apparently, Pam passed out and then fell, not the other way around.

Ben headed towards the bathroom and almost made it before he started throwing up. Ben had that just came out of prison, he had that Aryan nation look with mussels ripping all over the place , only his dark brown hair gave him any connection to humanity. Which made it look that much funnier when he was on his knees throwing up. I lifted Pam on my shoulder and had to keep hold of the bottom of the wedding dress down with one hand so I could see. I always wondered how someone that was only a hundred and five pounds could drink so much. At least the marvel of modern genetics meant no hangover or kidney problems, she could go like this of two hundred years, lucky me.

Julie came over and gave him a little too long kiss on the lips. "I've always wanted to have my ass that close to your face, some woman get all the luck." And she smiled again.

"Now was that nice, it's obvious I won't be consummating this marriage tonight. Did you have to make it worse by having me think about your ass all night?"

"You know what misery loves…."

"Yeah, anyway, dinner for the four of us when we get back?"

"Of course, now you better hurry, take it from me, warm vomit down your back it a horrible experience."

I took Pam back to our room room, removed the dress and noticed the Victoria secret outfit underwear, the thigh highs where snagged but it still was nice even though red on a redhead was not the way I would have picked. I plopped her on the bed and covered her up, stared at her for a min and for the first time consciously asked myself what the fuck am I doing?

I got a cigar from on top of the books I brought with me. Pam always said I spent more time in books then she ever did drinking so we were even. She kept asking way I was bring some on our honeymoon, it's funny how the drunks never know their drunks. I

went out to the tiny little patio and sat on a very uncomfortable chair and lit a cigar. I was watching swimmers in the flop. Air pushing the pool water up into the air until the water was a big water drop flying 3 stories in the sky and with a light ball in the center changing colors . There was always swimmers in the flying pools, how could you not like it. Far on the other side of the hotel I could see another fire from a cigarette on another tiny patio, it was Julie, and I could see the fire moving as she waved so I waved back. I sat there for a few hours smoking my cigars taking in the humid Florida air, listening to my newlywed bride snoring like a sailor and wondering what Julie was thinking about. I've always like 3:00am, it always felt like the darkest time of the night, the time when the darkness seems holy, mystical, of course I never told anyone that.

"What the hell?"

It was lights, I could see lots of flashlights from inside Julies and Ben's room then I herd a boom, it was the front door of the my hotel room exploding inward. Rushing behind the fragments of wood where men, lot of men in swat uniforms. When your poor you don't have a lot of options for DNA modifications, you have kind of basic templates that you can chose from. My dad, picked gentlemen for me, a sort of liberal arts major in DNA. My mom told me he wanted me to be a well rounded person, a real person. Not like the freaks running around now. At first I thought dad just picked the cheapest thing on the menu, as always..

When I was 12 I got my ass kicked by one of those warrior templates, they same type I'm sure rushing into my hotel room, so I decided to do something about it. When I was 16 , I became a mixed martial arts freak before there was M&A, mixing Kung-fu and western wresting, It was then that I saw the wisdom of my father, I could spare and go read books by Dumas, the other guys in the ring couldn't.

This all came as a big surprise to the men rushing in the room. The first one was running so fast towards me that I simply moved to the side and stuck my arm out which put me in the perfect spot to squat down put my arm under the second guys balls lift him up and body slammed him into the pretty glass coffee table. This gave me a little opening so I ran straight into the hallway threw the what was left of front door and turned around. If the wanted me now they would have to come through the door way and only one could fit at time Pam, was sleeping through all of this.

Ingratitude is an alcoholic.

There where 6 guys left standing in the room and 5 pulled out tasers, I was done. The six one put up his hand the guns went down and he slowly made it to the door way. Seems he wanted to do this old school, I can respect that coming from the Bronx, he was making small shuffling steps to the door, interesting.

He starts with a couple of jab probing really, no power to them, I move my head and move into the door way and kick his knee hard, he goes down to one knee and I bring my heal up to my shoulder and ax kick him on the collier bone, I hear the break and his scream at the same time. Then white pain, someone left in the hallway, electricity spasms across my body, followed by a rain of first and boots and that smell of my own blood in my nose before I fall into the black.

In prison, those things withheld and denied the prisoner become precisely what he wants most of all.

*Eldrige Cleaver.*

I'm creature of habit so I smiled a little as I heard the sound of Pam throwing up. This meant that it was about 4:30 am and today she wouldn't drink,be all healthy and sweet for a day. On top of that we should be heading out to the airport pretty soon, for our honeymoon, but the bed was really cold.

I jumped up to my feet, hands up and ready to fight as the flood of memories hit me. I felt my face that had been on the cold concrete floor start to warm up."

So the tough guy is awake, you were quite a surprise for us. We sent all the real hard asses to your friends room, I mean he looks like a convict. We sent the rookies to yours. Were did you learn all that stuff?"

"Who are you and why is it that when anything bad in the world happens it involves a short man." That spasm electrical again and I'm back on the floor in the fetal position. While I'm there I feel some boots kicking me but the pain of my whole body being electrocuted kind of dulling that pain.

After a while a hand reached down to help me up, it was Julie, as I stood up and took a look around the room I noticed that Julie stayed right next to me, not backing off like she normally did. The room was like a high school classroom with the same backboard and some unconvertible chairs and everywhere there was couples. Each kind of holding each other for support, some of the guys and two of the woman where bloody, it looks like I wasn't the only one to put up a fight.

Then the short man started talking again, he looked and sounded like a collage English lit teacher. I couldn't help notice his team of hoods, each with a different uniform. I could almost see him reading Keats out loud to his group of Special Forces wannabes while they torture some couple.

"So are we all finished with the jokes? Good, I have a dinner date tonight. First, as you can tell you have had your clothes changed, this is for your protection, some of you would stand out a little to much in NYC and you don't want that.. Ladies I'm sorry if you have some smelling or some bruising between your legs, but I can't control all my men and boys will be boys."

From the back of the room "Mother fucker." And a chair came flying at the little man, he moved out the way and I could see an African American woman running towards him. Then gun shots, lots and lots of gun shots, even when the woman was down, still more bullets a he man raced to protect her and got the same. The bullets kept flying until they didn't look like people anymore, just meat with some clothes on. We had all ran to the corners of the room when the gunfire started but one of the woman in the room still got hit with a ricochet in the leg.

No one moved to clean up the bodies or the blood that slowly spreading across the whole floor. Pam kept throwing up and now she was joined by 6 or 7 people and one woman who pissed on herself. All which gave the room a stench of death, the vomit, blood, piss and raw fear combining into something that couldn't be ignored.

But the short man kept talking. ....

"Like I was saying, each couple has it's own number for identification. Each person will be given a knapsack with one shot gun, two hand guns water and some food rations. Also, there is a detailed map of Manhattan island, which is were you are, in each bag." He lit a cigar, a punch, not a bad cigar but nothing fancy, actually I was glad he did as it took some of the edge of the smell in the room.

"You must all try to get off the island by walking across George Washington Bridge. If you try to take a cab, a train or a bike we will kill you. Only one couple will be allowed to make it across the bridge alive. Also, as far as the world is concerned, you no longer exist, every little bit of date, from the tiny toes on your birth certificates has been removed, your past bing dead, your just like shadows now."

Another drag "You have 12 days to make it to the GW bridge, if you haven't made it by then you will be killed., any questions?"

Another African American woman in the back, a tough looking one this time.

"Yeah, why the fuck are we here? What is this all about?"

"Oh you mean why you?" He took another drag.

"You where selected totally at random, just 12 couples from around the country who had been married within the last five years. So I guess you can consider yourself lucky."

Her man had gold teeth and the Crips tattoo on his hand.

"What if more then one couple makes it the bridge?""

That question woke me from my shock, this guy was already into tactical mode and I better get in the game now. I looked at Ben and he caught it to.

"Only one couple will be allowed across the bridge, so if more then one make it to the bridge, it's your problem.."

A beautiful blond with fuck me tits on my right spoke up.

"What if we don't want to do this..?"

"Then we kill you."

"I have one more question."

"Another wise crack and it'll be your blood getting all dry on the floor." At that someone starting throwing up.

"I think what was asked before was why your are doing this at all not just way us."

The little shit smiled.

"Oh I see. Well I can't really say, but if you that make it, and so far no comedians ever have, you will find out everything."

One of the guys in green uniform walked over "Sir 20 mins left"

"Ok listen up everyone, you have 15mins to get yourself prepared, after that you will be released and the competition will begin."

I walked over to Ben, Pam and Julie followed. Pam looked like some of the color was coming back to her face. Julie didn't look up she was busy securing her backpack and guns, once and awhile jumping up and down to make sure she could run with them. Which made here huge tits look even bigger and made me wonder how I could notice something like that with two people rotting on the floor.

I looked away and glanced over at our little jailer, he looked really young, maybe 40 if that. These days they are millions of modifications that can be made to DNA before child is born. Yet someone, somewhere went with short asshole, fascist bastard, man someone really didn't want to have him. But thinking of it gave me the answer, there were no parents, some board somewhere decided they needed on of those and here he is.

"Ben?"

"Yeah I saw it, I think the min they let us go we run as fast as we can away from the rest of the group. Problem is I don't anything about Manhattan."

"I know the upper east, lived there for a while." Of course what she really meant was she knew where all the bars and the local drug splicer dealers were.

"I know the city, and I bet we are someone down town."I said that with a lot of authority, but not a lot of facts.

"How did figure that?" Julie was always fascinated by my thought process, I don't know why.

"If they want us to get up to get to the GW Bridge, the farthest point would be downtown."

"Sure, "Ben wasn't convinced but it didn't really matter at this point, he was bouncing up and down now also.

"What the fuck are you guys talking about?" Pam's brain was still in hangover mode.

"It's like this baby; the little shit said that only some one of us are going to be allowed to make it across the bridge."

"So?" Hangover mind.

"So by the look in the homeboys eyes he's thinking of thinning out the herd a little to give himself better odds."

Julie helped "So we make sure our gear is strapped on tight to run, because homie is going to be busy for awhile. Some of these people are going to freeze some, like that couple over there looking at the map like there are on vacation, are going to get it to late and some will just scramble."

"What don't we just shoot them first?" from the mouths of babes.

"Pam I didn't know you had it in you. If we get into a firefight here close quarters with a lot of amateurs with guns one of us is going down.' Ben knows his stuff, I was just hoping not to have to kill innocent people, unless I had to.

"10 mins"

"Ben I know you were in the reserve and my dad loved skit shooting so we are OK, Pam?"

"Brothers and cousins took me dear hunting."

"Julie?"

"Lots of halo5000 on xbox680 holographic."

"Niiice." OK so we run, stay in a pack but not on top of each other. Now most likely I will know where I am but if you see a way out scream "clear" and start running and we will all follow. Keep one of the hand guns coked and at your side, anyone tries to stop you shoot. Pam did you hear me Pam?"

Pam was as close as a pacifistic as anyone I knew, so I grabbed her by the shoulders.

"Pam, what do you do if anyone tries to stop you."

She looked down

'I shoot them."

Right then gun shots started, we all hit the floor.

When it was all over three more couples were dead and one of the guards. You couldn't

stand in the room now without standing in blood. I guess a some people tried to make a break for it or those sadistic assholes got board

"2mins ,get ready.

One of the guards counted out the two mins out loud, it felt like the a million years. In that time I looked into the eyes of the of all people in the the room.

Most of the eyes where terrified, some looked lost but a few here and there had the eye of survival, these were the ones I had to watch..

"FIVE." One of the woman, Japanese I think, was crying and her hands were shaking, she had her knapsack , but she couldn't bring herself to pick up the guns, her man was yelling at her to get it done, it wasn't helping.

"FOUR" Another couple, one that had gone what weird twin thing, had there looks altered to look as much alike as possible were saying prayers. They where banging the floor which meant they were followers of the all powerful machine that they believe we are all part of..

"THREE"A guy in the back who looks like opie is slowly pissing in his pants.

"TWO" My mouth get really dry.

"ONE" A adrenalin dump that we all have when the modern body is shocked into life and death mode. Your senses are heighten you muscles tense and time is malleable.

The wall on one side slid open, that's when I and everyone else in the room, knew we were in a POD. Created after some Seattle Bushido cult pumped poison gas into the streets of Seattle. Home land security built millions of these pods all over the U.S.. You were suppose to run to them when the alarmed sounded. But they never explained the thinking behind them or what military department had recommended them and no one believed they worked. Eventually, as they aged and everyone forgot about them what they created was a fortified interconnected complex for every criminal in the continent. If you had any sense you made sure you day consists of never passing any of these den of thieves and murderers.

The room had been lit only by some table lamps and cheap florescent bulbs over head, so it took my eyes a few seconds to adjust to the light that filled the room. When they did I knew where we where , We were on the path train platform in downtown Manhattan. Which is the same as every other train platform in the world except a little sadder because it was totally rebuilt fast after the trade center was destroyed, then rebuilt again even cheaper with the roll out of the Mag-trains. Rebuilt with that forced modern look that barley hides it's own shabbiness. I could tell by the people on the platform it was about three o'clock, you had a lot of brain templates and a couple of worker templates, the cheapest template you can buy for your children. They are built for menial work for hundreds of years. It's no surprise that a lot of criminals come from that template base..

"CLEAR!" I yelled it as loud as I could.

I started running to the steps right in front of me and Pam, Ben and Julie were right behind me. A couple next to us tried to keep up with us and slipped on the blood, fell right on their faces, that is were the homeboy started. Shot them in the back of the head with the nine millimeter. This got all the commuters on the platform running and screaming which was good for us because our feet had just hit the steps. I spun around fired a shot gun blast over their head to get

them all running the other way This put them all right into
the homie that was pumping non stop all around him to
get anyone. His woman was sitting down on the platform
pumping her shotgun at about knee height. The commuters
were getting mowed down.

The couple was fantastic the precision of there shots was
almost poetic, it was always hart shot, a head shot, liver, one
shot and dead. They fired like the ammo was worth more
then the people they were killing.

We all ran up to the stop of the and stopped, I grabbed
Pam's arm.

"What the fuck?" I still was supposed with beautiful
woman when they cursed, I found the contrast so sexy.

"How many are left?"

"What?"

How many of the couples are left?"

Pam has photographic memory, part of her template,
she would have remembered every couple that was in the
POD with us and could instantly tell me how man where
left alive.

"11 , lefts get out of here."

The homie was starting at me, he hadn't noticed me as
a real enemy in the POD, now he did.. I head a shot right by
my ear and turned to see Julie with a smoking 9mm.

"I just don't like him."

"Nice, Ben no wonder you drink so much."

"Asshole." The last thing you should tell a drunk is that
he drinks to much.

We ran straight to Broadway and into a star bucks, which
normally has the most self absorbed people in the world, a
perfect place to talk with no one listing.

> God put me on this earth to accomplish a certain number of things. Right now I'm so far behind that I will never die.

> *Bill Watterson.*

Jan's dad worked for CSXHS railroad all her life and on every vacation since she was 5 he would take the whole family to see at least one High speed train track or yard. The family visited HSPATH train in NYC or as he called in the port authority trans Hudson rail, about 5 years ago, In dads opinion the Path wasn't really a high speed train, it could only get up to 150miles per hours which was nothing compared to the monsters going from NYC to Orlando at 700 miles per hour. But since the system was small he liked it anyway.. As always he had the maps downloaded weeks in advance and the whole family talked about every stop and engineering, choice made. Jan liked the tunnels, where the real action was. Sometimes the rest of the family zoned out but anything her father did was wonderful. So Jan knew exactly what to do when the guy with the gold teeth starting shooting. She grabbed her husband's hand and jumped off the platform onto the tracks

"Come on Robert, run!"

Her husband Robert ran track in high school, that is were they met, so the run into the darkness of the tunnel was nothing for them. They had keep running all these years, but also they both had, new Cirval contacts which give them night vision, while making their eye's balls a cool gray. The eyes also, displayed constant time and could access TV and the Internet feed directly to the eyes. Jan's knew if they kept running this tunnel would take them ,like it did millions every day, into New Jersey. One of her eyes had a little blue print of the tunnel right at the bottom of her sight. When they got to NJ they would head straight to the airport, the planes where slow but cheap and no one checked security on airplanes, only nobodies took them now, like the old greyhounds buses.

" Robert don't run in the middle, stick close to the sides in case a train comes".

Then it came, the mag trains are as quite as the wind and are called wind snakes in china. In the USA they added a high pitch sound to them when they are away from the platforms, in case someone is on the tracks. You don't really need it for the path, the blast of wind rushing threw the tunnel hits you like a hurricane. They both found a little workers alcove and strapped themselves in and waited.

When a train passes you at 100 miles and hour it's not like a regular train, you don't get a glimpse of the people as the windows pass in front of you. What you see is one quick flash of light as you eyes, even Jan,s new eyes, see the whole train in a second. In that second Jan thought she saw something like those old horror movies were that flash a horrible sight in front of your eyes for a second, to scare your subconscious. In that second she thought she saw,. in the alcove directly across from her, eyes, yellow cat eyes.

When your in a tunnel and a magtrain passes by your ears take a while to adjust. So for a while Robert and Jan didn't hear anything except there own harts pounding from the running. Then slowly they started to hear things, water from broken pipe, the sounds of other trains in other tunnels. As they kept running they started to hear something that was out of place in a subway tunnel. At first they both ignored it, thought it was the ringing of their ears. Then logic kicks in there feet slow down and they look at each other and slowly turn around.

"What is that?" Robert knew but he wouldn't admit it to himself, but it screamed in his mind.

"Lion, no doubt."

Robert had a summer job in the local neo-zoo when he was a kid, that was more then a hundred years ago and designer hybrids were just coming out. Everyone was mixing animals of all types and his job was to feed the animals in the lion+ exhibit. He knew the sound of hungry lions they low rumbling growl that you feel more then hear, even if you mix the lion with a monkey.

They still couldn't see it and they were both using their contacts to scan every conceivable spectrum of light and every web cab in the tunnel. Then they saw both saw the eyes, yellow eyes with no body. Robert looked at the eyes, he had seen lion eyes hundreds of times and there was something wrong with these something he couldn't place.

"Robert run!!!"

He ran, they both did, he knew there was no way they could outrun it, so he waited until they were both at full speed and then he stopped pivoted and ran towards it. Robert and Jan were pacifist, they didn't take the guns that the little man had offered them. . As he was running back he remembered his life before Jan, it was like looking at old black and white photos, more like a documentary then real life, Jan brought color life laughter into his life. All he could think of was saving that bit of magic for the world if not for himself. Finally he could see what was wrong with the eyes on the lion thing they where two high up and a little to small like the eyes were of a man. It lunged at Bob and ripped out his throat with lion claws on human hands, it seems the lions+ had come a long way since he was a kid.. Jan had turned around and saw Bob running away from her she ran after him just time to see him decapitated.

"No.." The lion man looked at her and smiled with too many teeth.

The little man is Tom Orchard. Tom turned around from the monitors and headed back to his office. The rest of the men kept watching screams of that woman started to excite the men in the room.. Tom closed the door behind him and slumped down on his desk, he wondered how men could watch someone get raped and eaten by a half man half lion and consider it entertainment.

Remi entered the office without knocking, he never knocked. Every person on this project worked for a branch of the government. Tom worked for the executive branch. Everyone except Remi he worked for Davos group. They were only here to advise, but no one was kidding themselves, the Davos group was the new Illuminati they watched everything. If anyone crossed them, president, movie star, business man, you could expect a horrible death and to be wiped out from every database in the world.

"You don't like porno?"

Tom took a drag, "Not into beasts, besides it doesn't help the project." Remi squinted his eyes, just a little, which would probably be a disappointment to his Davos teachers.

"No, I understand you don't like porno of any kind in fact you don't have any vice I can find in your file."

Tom blew a big puff of smoke to Remi's face, "Really, none?"

"Tom, please don't underestimate us, many have, and died, we know you just started smoking a few years ago. A little late to pick up a vice, maybe it is really just a smoke screen to through us off the track and because you think your funny."

"Yeah, maybe, but I have a question for the illuminated ones why don't you get rid of sex drive when you make you hybrids?"

"To deep in the DNA, without lust they wouldn't be human. Call me when we have the next encounter."

Maybe,,or maybe you like to remove everything you can't control but leave the rest in.

The Davos group ruled by controlling people's vices, entertainment, drugs, sex, if you didn't have a vice you came up on there radar. Tom knew this more then most because last summer he took a drive out to Amish country, like his family did when he was a kid. His dad liked to getaway not only from the city but from the century. Tom couldn't find the Amish he found little mc-mansion, martin bars, and condos, but no Amish. He knew the Davos group did it there was no news of it. "Fucking red shirts.."

He leaned back and stared at the last moments of Roberts life, saw the look on his face as he ran to what he knew was his death. He saw, as he had many times before, the face of love.

"A crappy plan today is better then a
hole in the head tomorrow" —

"A coffee shop, there are people shooting at us and you take us into a coffee shop?" Ben wasn't happy but even I had to agree people shooting at you is a good reason to go to a bar.

"Yeah, yeah I'm asshole, you sound like my wife, now say you're to tired and want to go straight to bed."

Julie laughed and Pam hit me on the back of the head.

"I just wanted us to make a plan first."

I picked starbucks because the people in these places are so self absorbed you could plan the over throw of the world, complete with the genocide of vast sections of humanity with thermal nuclear weapons and no one would here would care as long as it didn't impact the spring fashion line.

"So what's the plan baby?" Pam was using her let's flatter the man and make him feel good so we could get to the drinking voice

"Yes, baby, what plan?" Pam and Julie just looked at each other.

"Well I assuming since they gave us 12 days to make a walk that we could finish in a day and some pretty serious firepower for free I'm guessing the walk is going to be interesting ."

"So?"

Ben's "so?" was what I expected.

"So what do you have in mind suicide, we go underground, magic what?" Julie was just having fun now.

"I tell you what we shouldn't do, we shouldn't take the shortest route to the bridge."

"OK now you're just being a pain in the ass. You bring us in here to make a plan, which you don't have. Then you tell us we should make ourselves an even bigger target by taking the long way out of here. I say we get the fuck out of here and find a string of bars all the way to the GW Bridge."

Ben got up and headed to the door and the sad part was that Pam got up with him. I was going to say something but I caught something out of the corner of my eye, a man running. Now in downtown Manhattan a man running is not that odd, but he seem to be running right at us.

He ran straight into the window where all the beautiful people were sitting, crashing in and spraying glass on everyone. I squatted and so did Ben pulling Julie and Pam down with us. I took a look at the running man and noticed his hair; he had long gold hair, not blond, gold and weird eyes. He started coming at us, then the manager of the place got in his face. The guy picks him up by the throat and squeezed until he was dead. Most of the people had ran out during those minutes but we were pinned because I thought sitting way in the back was more discreet. Ben started shooting at him with one of the hand guns, but the guy had a weird bullet proof vest on him. The bullets weren't just being stopped by the vest they were being sent back at us. I threw one of tasteful chairs at him which knocked him back and gave us a little room we ran around him and all started firing at him and more bullets started coming back at us.

"What the fuck is going on?"

I still was waiting for Ben to make a sentence without the word fuck but he have a point, then the guy jumped at me. I rolled out of the way but my hands still got cut up and I lost my gun. The rest of the gang keep shooting and the guy kept smiling with those big teeth then he jumped at Julie. Julie switched to the shotgun, which still didn't stop him but the slugs went all over the place one finally got me in the arm. Julie fell to the floor and he was on top of her in a second, she was barely holding it back with her hands around it throat. I ran up behind it and shot it in the temple point blank in fell right on Julie, hard.

"Baby.. ... what took you so long?" Julie gave me a sly smile and even the dead guy knew what it meat.

"Hey Julie, you need to back up." Pam was getting a little sick of Julia's wit, she would remember it when she was drunk.

"Sure... Can someone get this guy off me, he smells a little gamely,"

"Well you wanted a man on top of you, didn't you?" Like I said Pam was getting tired of Julia wits.

"Come on help me get him off I need a drink." Ahhh Ben, if nothing else alcoholics are focused.

I helped Ben get the guy off Julie and waited as the rest of my group started to argue about what to do now, apparently now we needed a plan. They kept arguing as I started to move over the glass towards the door and I kept remembering Calligans law, You can't argue with stupid. But walking out of Starbucks, I notice how some of the fashionable people had fallen on top of each other as they died, It looked so intimate, ironic for this crowd.

"Maybe we should start with getting out of here because if the cops arrest us we can't get to the bridge on time."

They all looked at me and all started walking..

"Nice call, baby" For the first time I noticed that I hated when Pam called me baby.

We made it water street under the Brooklyn bridge and into china town. Witch had over the years swallowed up little Italy, some of Soho and made it across the Manhattan bring to eat up some of downtown Brooklyn. It was always under construction, there was always a newer bigger building going up. Right then another couple runs past up with 9mm in there hand, Pam screams out.

"They are heading to the bridge."

"Mother fuckers.."

Ben started chasing them, I don't know why, I doubted he knew why but we all started running after Ben who was running after them. Then the male was flatten into the ground by a snake arm. In 2020, there was a freak accident in Mexico City, near hurricane winds toppled over a construction crane which went into a mosque which just happens to be having a big meeting of all the clerics from Mexico and South America, 100 died and the Muslims in Mexico and all of south America rioted for 3 weeks. All over the world Muslims attacked construction cranes and put a fatwa on them.

There was no convincing them that inanimate objects could not have a "crusade against Islam" after that no one would insure the cranes. Since then the "snakes" have taken over. They look like big square trailers with huge metal snakes coming out of them each snake can reach up to 20 stories tall and when a building is bigger they just put one every 20 floors and work up. Each are preprogrammed for the job they have to do so there is never human error and they are hundreds of times safer them the old cranes. In all the years that the snakes have been in use there has never been even one accident. So I there no reason to believe that that man flatten on the street was the first accident ever.

The woman who had just seen her husband smashed was frozen in place screaming with piss streaming down her pants. We all watched transfixed as the same snake arm that had crushed the bones of her husband slowly undulating up about 5 stories up. Then Ben started shooting at it with his shotgun, over and over again, the snakes where about as thick as a couch and made of a kind of super titanium. So there was nothing he could do, or anyone could for that matter. It went right through the sidewalk and didn't slow down as it went past the screaming woman. I looked up and saw other snakes slowly rising and knew that we were all dead, we couldn't out run them and we couldn't stop them. I started shooting at them with the 9mm, just wanted to go down fighting.

Then I felt something, on my shoulder shaking me hard it was Pam and she was shooting something all I heard was follow me, RUN! The all four of us were up against the control cab, the one place where the snakes couldn't reach. That's when the adrenalin dump starts and time comes flowing back to all my senses.

"Does anyone have any ideas..?" I still had to yell, this time over the noise or the snakes; they were clearly pissed off because they couldn't get to us.I looked over and Julie was frozen looking that the pool of blood and the little bits of meat that was Mrs. 33. Pam was on the other side of Ben so

I barely heard her scream "we have to get into the control cab and destroy it inside."

There was on small door that technicians used for service and we all started shooting at it at the same time. Pam was closest so when the door was mostly Swiss cheese she kicked to open. Then out came hundreds of tiny metal crabs, well they looked like crabs but they where maintenance drones. The little things took care of the whole platform, right now taken care of the platform meant getting rid of us. In seconds they were all over us, they are easy to smash with you boots, but a bitch to get out of your hair of out of pants if they get in. They were so small, twice as small as a real crab, they are more of a nuisance then a real deterrent. We kept sliding over to the door keeping our backs to the control cab and swatting and smashing the little crabs. Right in front of the door Ben falls down; one of the crabs had actually tied his laces together, smart fucks. Pam and I couldn't stop laughing, I actually dropped to my knees and was almost covered in the metal crabs. We made it inside and just started shooting until our clips were empty, I heard a long moment of complete silence, my ears rang like I had been to a concert sitting right in front the speakers for 4 hours then walking out into the dark night. Then the sound of mountain falling, Pam and I were knocked down by the impact of whatever it was. When we got back outside the snakes had all fallen down, some crashing thought the sidewalk, exposing pipes and endless wires. Julie walked over to the blood pool she had been staring at the whole time knelt down and pick out a small little sliver cross and put it in her pocket.

"Let's find a bar." I knew Julie for 7 years and had never heard her say that.

"Sure, let's keep moving uptown.

**Fighting for peace is like screwing for Virginity.**

*George Carlin*

We stopped off at a pub in the beginning of Greenwich Village. Mostly Irish, and 99% percent white, my brother used to say the word pub means bar for white people. I being the I percent was drinking water and watching Julie who had said nothing and was doing shots of chilled vodka.

I moved a little close to her "So, you OK? What's up."

"Me, oh mad a god again."

"God?"

"Yeah it didn't bother me those people got in the little holding pen we were in or on the platform, even that guy that that got it smashed like a mosquito on someone's arm, didn't bother me."

"The woman?"

"Yeah, did you see her, frozen in place, peeing and crying and watching death coming down on her and she just stood there. I know it's the Adrenalin some run some people fight and some poor assholes just freeze. That's what pisses me off, I mean why would you put that in people, make it so they would freeze. It's like he said, this group is going to be my warriors this group is going to be my offices workers and this group, fuck em." I didn't have anything to say and I'm not sure she wanted me to, after a while I pointed to Ben and Pam that had got into a drinking game with Irish guys. Ben was getting most of it on his shirt at this point and Pam had one shot glass in each hand.

"Your funny, always on the big question never on the one that really matters."

"Like?"

"Like why the fuck we are here, being shot at, attacked by si fi mutants and of course what the fuck is on the other side of the GW bridge?"

"Yeah... When I go into denial I go big." She smiled and took another shot.

"There one thing that keeps bothering me, that lion guy. He just sought of stood there, mean for a couple of seconds there he had us. We were just kind of standing there with our mouths open."

"Yeah, your right and you where really close to the spot that woman got splattered, you were an easy target. I mean I have seen those things before and they can move when they have to."We both just sat quietly for awhile, we knew it meant something we just didn't know what."So you gave up drinking so Pam could drink more." "What? oh. I had a friend Joe, from Staten island, big island guy, could beet three guys in a fight and 10 in a drinking contest. Every time we would up at a pub he wouldn't drink, so one day I asked why, he told me the advice his father gave him. Irish people are great when there sober, but after a couple of shots it, ginny, nigger, spic or whatever to every one that isn't Irish. So if your in a pub you should be ready to fight."

"Come on, times have changed, you can't"

And just like we where all actors in some sitcom for the gods, a guy slides over to Julie. "Hey beautiful, what you doing with that Mexican, slumming. Hey boy should you be getting back to the kitchen?"

We both started laughing hysterically which made the guys bear muscles nearly explode and he pushed Julie. Julie was going to unload a full clip into him so I steped in. I had my hand in my pocket and a leathermen held in my fist light a brass knuckles I clock him with a hammer fist in the jaw and the mettle of the leather man breaks his jaw. Then the bar explodes. A bar fight is in many ways is really a work of art, I really believe if everyone could be in one at least once in there life, people would get along with each other a lot better. This particular bar fight, and they are all different like snow flakes, was perfect, the chairs where light enough to throw, there was only three guys in the bar that were really fights. These you could tell by there efficiency and they why they stepped from person to person. The woman where nicely mixed in and every one was equally drink, except for me.

And this bar fight was close to perfect, the guys where and whaling away, like drunks do. Julie was even putting some of them down. Pam and Ben where wrestling with a huge block of other drunks. Someone threw a chair at my head which missed, I noticed a petite little brunette with the fearless flawless lips flinging darks at woman's breast. One guy got hit in the stomach and starting puking creating a nice slippery pool which a nice couple that was trying exit without getting involved, slipped on it and was tried to crawl the rest of the way.

Then things got ugly, another couple sitting way in the back and talking while people where stating to bleed, opened up with shotgun. I dove to the floor and took Julie with me.

But they kept coming for us so we rolled and rolled until we found a pillar to hide behind. The Julie starting firing back with her 9mm which pushed them back a little. "Julie, keep shooting." I made ran towards the woman, who was the closest me, she got two shots of pump shotgun off. The buck shot hit me on the chest and bounced into hers. I was going to move on the guy but his head exploded as Ben and Pan open up on him, they kept firing on him as he fell to the ground and even a couple of shots after. The bar had emptied out after the first shot.

"What the fuck was that all about." It was good to know no matter how drunk Ben got he could still curse.

**The race is not always to the swift nor the battle to the strong, but that's the way I bet.**

*Damon Runyon*

Ziowan province in china was the best place in the world to have a martini a Cuban cigar and a hooker. It used to be Vegas, one day gambling was outlawed in all of the USA, in 10 years all the casinos went black. Some of the retailers tried to hang on but eventuality they gave up. It took another five years before all the millions of small overpriced ranchers were empty, the lucky ones sold early, the less lucky sold at a lost, the miserable's lost here Jobs and left in th middle of the night from a house thaws being foreclosed. Now no one goes to Vegas unless it's on the way to somewhere else.

In Zaiwan province there are more Americans than anywhere else in the world, tonight 20 of them are on top of the casino called the colbot dragon. From the penthouse windows 50 stories up you can see all the lights of ziowan province stretch out as far as the eye can see. You could also just make out the tips of the 2 100 foot colbot dragons that stride the roof, there eyes shooting out four rotating 10,000 candle watt lights into the sky. They say if you stood on the moon you could see there eyes but they say a lot of things in ziowan province.

In the penthouse there are two very large very expensive conference tables. One a little over 500 million dollars in cash from all over the world, some in gold coins some diamonds some gems and some25,000 dollar chips from the casino down stairs. It also had one heavy armed person at each point of the table, two of the guys were supplied by the casino and two were hired just for this job. There was another two outside the door of the room standing on the colbot rug that also lead to the elevator doors that have two more guards. Not that anyone or thing was coming up because the elevator was shut down there was armed men in the lobby outside the hotels on every roof around the casino helicopters in the air which has had all it's air traffic diverted.

The second table has 22 monitors on it 14 were shut of and the rest were had a number which represents the odds the bookers were giving and how much money had been put down. The bottom had a scrolling ticker of where the couple was in real time and snippets of there life. In the other room there was 34 people of very ages and nationalities. They were all looking at some huge monitors that should really be in a base ball stadium not in a hotel. They were watching all the action shots of the couples being killed.

"I like the bar shoot out, but the girl getting boned while he's eating her like Tatar. That's entertainment."

No one knew how old Pedro was, he was one of the first people on the planet to get DNA corrective drugs. When they first made these things there were unstable and had a lot of side affects. But drugs that can extend you life for an undermined amount of time are well worth the risk. As far as Pedro was concerned nothing with a payoff that great can come without a cost. Which most people believe explains Pedro's on again off again bouts of madness. The drugs are much more refined now but the damage has been done.. Pedro favorite saying was "The devil knows more because he is old then because he is the devil". No one know who was older, the devil or Pedro, neither one was telling.

Ziowan, like Vegas before, would bet on anything and everyone sports, politics, even the weather. They even took up the dark bets, like bets on homicide rates in Philly, dead pools and even bets on body counts and winners and losers of the last genocide. Today's action was sweet because it was suppose to be so secretive so it was illegal on so many levels. Betting wise it was easy, you could see all the couples before they start and what the book makers odds are. You picked a couple and put at least 2million Amerazone down. If you bet right you could walk always with everything on the big tab plus the house would have to settle up with you if you took long odds. Last year the winner walked away with 1.5 billion. Unfortunately his only daughter and living relative emptied out an entire clip into his head right in the lobby of the casino. Once the brain has been destroyed like that there is nothing anyone can do and she was in charge of his clones, he never made it back. She never did a day in jail, seems no one saw a thing and all the cameras were turned off at the time. She own a small casino down the street from the Colbot Dragon now. Rumor has it that she has a computer that has her fathers brain dumped on it and she likes to play mahjong with him once and awhile.

"Well kids, poppie, has to pee, which one of you little toy soldiers is going to join me?"

Everyone who made a bet was locked in the penthouse, fed by the finest chefs in the world, they slept on silk sheets and even provided company via various pleasure templates, The young ladies and gentleman had to be blind and deaf to make it to the beds and they knew they would be filmed, the casino made sure it was worth there while. There were no phones in the room and no cell phones were allowed but just to be sure all the signal were scrambled. All and all a better real world example of a golden cage could not be found anywhere else in China. Pedro said it himself, "Who in this room hasn't killed someone for a lot less then what is in that table?"

Pedro and his two baby sitters went to the bathroom were he unzipped and started peeing in the gold, not gold plated, urinal. He held the flusher and taped it with his index finger. The colbot dragon has just been completed 2 months ago, but Pedro had been working for this moment since the first formal announcement that the hotel was going to be build. He hired 500 different contracts from 100 different countries, each with a tiny little part to build and none of them knowing what the other was doing. All that work, about 50 million Amerizone's to install a cable to the penthouse bathroom with a switch that can't be seen or felt. You just had to know the right spot to Tap and he did, he just tapped the Morse code, which no one used anymore and in a coffee shop in NYC a cell phone receives a tripled encrypted message full of I's and zero's. Pedro looked over to the guards

"When you've been peeing for a 300 hundred years then you can look at me like me"

Perdro headed back to the room with the rest of the gamblers and ordered himself a blow job and some sushi.

On a napkin in NYC the little ones and zero's are translated into."Why the fuck weren't you at the bar, that was to close. I'm not paying you to vacation in NYC, if you can't get it done I can send in someone else.

20 blocks up from the little phone couple 6 is in a very mahogany room in the upper east side. Couple six came from two very rich and very powerful families and they came straight here once they were set lose. This was a brownstone that belonged to the woman's mother, mom was in the us senate as was the husband brother. The Woman's dad ran a private banking group based out of Switzerland and last estimate net worth was in the billions. The mans mother and father wealth was unknown since most of it was inherited, however it was known that his father controlled the docs in Japan. Not an easy thing to do for a westerner.

All four parents came into the room at the same time, they stood there latterly with there mouths open listing to the story there children told. You could feel that the literal personification of wrath materializing right there in the room. Then when the story was of adduction, imprisonment, subjugation was told there all stood there for a few incredible slow seconds in silence. Which was only broken by the sounds of the parents heads exploding like kids putting m80's in watermelons.. But instead off the happy summer like pulp of watermelon being splattered all over the clothes and sneakers and baseball caps of laughing boys and girls. It was the brains and blood of there very own parents that now covered them. But what the man will never forget was seconds later when the bodies off these people who they loved who they depended on, who were movers and shakers hit the 20,000 dollar rugs like meat thrown from a meat hook.

They screamed, for what seemed like hours, there body rocking from the force. Then they dropped to there knees and fell to there faces and cried the blood that the rug soaked up was still warm an it got on there faces. Hours, years, , who can mark the time of grief and despair, what man made time piece can record it. They eventually move, like zombies to find the butler dead, the cleaning lady dead the doorman dead. But it's the pugs that get them both, the force of the bullets that hit the pugs spread them across the walls. As they both stood there looking the man takes out a 9mm and shoot the woman in the head and then himself. Across the street as a team of snipers packs up the Sergeant walks over to Reyes and ask. "Why you kill the dogs?" "It was funny."

## The complete lack of evidence is the surest sign that the conspiracy is working.

We made it to 14 st and Union Square park, right when we get to the park entrance shots ring out. Funny thing is I don't flinch anymore, I'm like a war veteran now, just dive in the foxhole, what else id there to do. In out case we jumped behind one of those massive buses that roam the city like triceratops if triceratops had constantly shifting advertisements. I shot out 5 of the 50 wheels which was enough to kept the Eco-friendly dinosaur from moving.

"Ben, you see anything?"

"I got nothing, Pam?"

"Crazy, something crazy."she was seeing, feeling something we weren't yet.

I heard more guns different guns, not the type of guns I first heard and not coming our way, there was another player. Whoever or whatever it was it stopped the bullets coming our way. We stayed there for a few minutes looking for some better covert o move to , when Pam points to the subway. The new mag-trains couldn't run on the old tunnels so they had been converted to huge underground shopping malls. With chic little stores each representing the neighborhood they are in. and alone the tubes hydroponic gardens grew vegetables and fruit using solar light from the building above. I missed the trains and even thou everyone I know has told me I am wrong. I can swear I smell the faint whiff of homeless man urine.

I didn't want to make a go for the subway until we could at least see where the bullets where coming from. Looking around I see Loki's bookstore for all things dark, dead and devilish. The store has two three story tall Loki's guarding the door, I always wondered how the book shop got away with them because they where exact replicas of the Loki's in the marvel Thor comics. I suppose even the intellectual property attorneys have stopped reading along with everyone else.

But as I was lying there with my face pressed down against the concrete, I saw one of there heads move. The huge yellow mammoth shaped tusks suddenly running across the street and into the park, I taped Julie on the shoulder and pointed, every one looked and said nothing. I mean what would you have to say if you took the whole family, mom, dad and two kids to Washington and when your standing in front of the Lincoln memorial on a hot DC August day, with a soda in your hand and ice cream in the kids, what do you have to say when Lincoln gets up and runs across the park. I could see Loki gaining speed as it ran into the square, people ran but I hardly noticed them, I was getting used to people running wherever I was. Then the view of it's head was blocked by a tree for a second and we saw a body flying. It was moving upwards, arms flaying, up from the ground, across the street and into a third floor window.

"Let's get the fuck out of here". I absolutely fucking agree with you Ben!

I ran, we all ran west on14th street, trying to lose our self's in the hundreds of people that were running. As I'm running I notice a shadow flying over us, not a bird then I see another body without a building to stop it' downward trajectory. It falls right in front of us hitting the ground with that thud that I had heard before. I know the thud, because 5 years ago with Shari law was imposed in France, a group of Muslim boys took a bunch of French girls that weren't wearing Burkas and Christian, or whores to them, up to the top of the Eiffel tower. There dropping them off the tower one by one and becoming hero's in the Muslim umma. A few years latter they made a kind of rap record that was a call to murder Chinese and in the background they had sampled the thuds of the girls hitting the street as a back beat..

"What now?" There is more screaming behind us so we all turn around. Loki was coming down the street at full speed knocking people down with those huge horns.

We started running again and made it to eight st where we took the right hoping it would keep going, but it didn't it was after us. Sometimes when I'm really nervous I get the giggles this was one of those time. I started thinking about how people paid lots of money to be in Madrid and do this. The giggles usually proceeded an act of desperation on my part, and some times I would break into a song.

It was about half a block away from us when I stopped.

"Well let's give this a shot"

I pulled out my shotgun and started firing, it didn't kill or even make a little hole, but it did change its path I could tell I was hurting it and so could the others so they all opened up on it and pushed back around the corner. We kept running for another block or two, then I couldn't anymore. I stopped bent over trying to catch my breath and that's when it started raining boxes, wooden creates where coming down from the rooftops. The giant was throwing huge wooden crates at us over five story buildings. The boxes exploded on impact, shooting splinters everywhere like little wood missiles, I couldn't stop laughing.

"What's so funny?"

"Look what's in the boxes."

It was stuffed toys, they were going to kill us with stuff toys. I stopped laughing when the ram headed guy landed right in the middle of the street. It came right at us, really too fast to describe, we were able to jump away and it rammed right into the building. I got hit with flying bricks on my back slamming my face first on the concrete which I was kinda getting used to. Dizzy, I could see the thing stepping back from the building; I could finally see it up close. The massive back and neck the arms like tree trunks, legs.. legs were all wrong, everything else about the freak was red and yellow and huge and powerful. But the legs were all pink and soft, like the belonged to some out of shape guy from Germany. I looked around and everyone was on the ground Julie was out, Ben and Pam where crawling away, but I can't find a gun.

The thing turns around and look down at me picking me up by back collar like a little puppy, it's eyes are red with yellow pupils. It lifts me over its head and from 9 foot up I could see all the guns. He slams me on my back into the sidewalk right on top of one of the 9mm, which now feels like it's going to pop out my stomach. I can't breathe and there is warm blood coming out of my mouth. My vision is blurring but I could still see yank up Julie and Ben, throwing them across the street into a store window.

Pam was next but things went different this time, it bent down and spent some time looking at her. Well I knew this thing was a male now, Pam had that same effect on every male. His peep show gave let me time catch my breath roll over and put a bullet in his odd legs. It screamed and screamed again until it went down to its knees. I ran over and put gun right on it's forward head.

"WAIT" it's voice was rough like a gravel.

"Why.?"

"I CAN HELP, I WANT TO HELP." The others were getting up and I could hear Ben cocking the shotgun.

"So, talk what can you offer" I was going to kill it but what was the hurry, maybe I could get something out it first/

"INFOMATION."

"Well, you better come up with a sample, I don't like promises"

"WACHING YOU, HAVE CAMERAS ON YOU ALL TIME LISNTING".

That made Ben turn away from the thing and start pointing his shot gun up, looking for cameras, it made a lot of sense to me.

"So, you can't help with that."

"YES, CAN. HAVE FOOD, WATER SAFE PLACE AMMO"

"We are running out of ammo" Pam was always counting every penny, knew the cost of everything.

"Ok, do it."

It moved fast to the middle of the street and lifted up the manhole cover and threw it down the street. I kept my gun on him the whole time and the way he flung that 100 pound manhole cover made me reconsider my deal.

"COME THIS WAY."

We all looked at each other but we all wound up heading down the hole, I mean we didn't have a lot of options.

Bad news always look worse on monitors, this time was no different for Tom. As he watched two of the couples and an expensive mutant go underground. Away from their cameras into a world where the walls are so thick with concrete and cables and pipes that no tracking device on the planet would work he took a look at his little friend with the red shirt and wondered how long it would take him to try to blame him for this.

"So what are you going to do now?" Turned out is was only 5 seconds.

"What am I going to do? That fucking freak was a your creation, looks like you "New World Order" assholes are just and dickless and incompetent as all the other police state child rapers from the UN you replaced. I have an idea, something that might be really alien to you, why don't work on finding a solution to the problem instead of trying the blame it on the closest dick you can find" The room went quiet, there was a story about a Davos that went to the UN to outlaw the word pussy, just because someone called him one. If it wasn't for the fact that the head of the UN board of languages liked to scream fuck my pussy at the top of her lungs when she was helping the poor boys of Haiti he would have go it done.

"You will never work again, this time next year you'll be eating rats for dinner."

"Yeah, the way your boys fucked the US economy there is probably Russian school crossing guards that make more than me already."

These red shirts where very touchy and Larry knew that this little blow out together with red shirts latest Lego DNA job going missing would distract him from the video. He wouldn't even notice the high powered rifle fire that someone was firing at one of the couples on 14$^{th}$ st. He wouldn't ask Larry who it was and he wouldn't have to answer, It was a question he didn't have an answer to.. Larry walked out the room and headed to the bathroom, to the one stall that didn't have a camera in it because one of his men pissed on it. The kid who must have had a world class prostrate to hit it with a piss steam up on the ceiling.

He called my field team sergeant Harry.

"Yeah?"

"Where are you?"

"C's" C's" A cheap frat house bar in lower Manhattan, under the entrance ramp of the Brooklyn Bridge. It had lot of bras hanging from the ceiling, that was a rule at the c's. If you had a c cup or bigger and put it on the ceiling you would drink free.

"We have a new player."

"Where?" As he was asking he made a little circle with his index finger and 5 men put 20 dollars on the table and moved to the door.

"Last spotted on 14st using a high powered rifle, I'll get video if I can and put it your memory site.."

"Do we know what the game is?"

"No, could be anybody."

"Who knows?"

"Just you and me for the next 24 hours and if want to get that fat consultant check at the end of this shit it better stay that way." Larry hung up and took a piss holding his dick with a shaking hand.

We are sitting on plastic milk crates our feet are wet from a constant stream of dirty water streaming past us and leaving a smell of old socks and dirty asses in it's wake. This is where the thing lived, no matter, it kept it's word, gave us food clean water and ammo. More importantly he had the latest and greatest in hardware, I traded up to a sonic shotgun. I liked the fact that on low a persons organs, all of them, would explode inside the body, no mess. On high the thing could stop a truck coming at you on the highway, and it weighed as much as an old 9mm.

"Were did you get all the beer?"

"Truck comes once a week for delivery to the stores around here I take a case."

We got drunk and started talking and laughing and having a good time.

"So what is your name?" I don't know, I felt bad for him or I felt that you can't be this good of a host and not have some humanity.

"Don't have one, I never talk to anyone so I don't really need one."

Everyone was quiet, we never heard of someone with no name, how far down the social ladder do you have to be to make a name useless.

"Well Ray, you have one now."

"Ray?"

"Yeah, Ray, it a good guy's name and you're a good guy."

Ben couldn't resist, "You guys need some time alone?"

We all smiled and kept drinking and eating and telling jokes. Ray didn't know how to tell jokes but he had endless stories of the human condition from his position on the wall, he was that one wall that did have ears.

Then I noticed it, I mean Ray, was staring at Pam and Pam was staring back.

"What?" Pam never liked being stared at.

"How was it to be a child?"

"What?"

"Five years ago I found myself here, watching that screen with a man giving me orders. Since then I found out everything I knew before that moment was implanted, put in my head. I know I was made, somewhere somehow. Not you, you were born, raised, loved by someone. How was it?"

Pam looked down at her beer.

"I'm sorry did I make you feel uncomfortable, I didn't mean to."

"When I was seven my father had a big four door sedan, a BMW 740I with a massive V8 engine that the UN hated even when they where legal. One perfect Sunday in May, you know the kind of perfect day you see in the background of paintings at the Met, it's 75 degrees, the birds sing the even the grass is perfect. After church we would head on home and mom would make us a nice lunch before she got too drunk. .But not this time, this time my farther went on the highway and opened up the big v8 and the sun roof. My brother and I looked up at the blue sky and pointed out the clouds that looked like candy, they all looked like candy to us then.. We made our way to the New Jersey botanicals gardens, where my brother and I ran in open fields and around hundreds of different kinds of flowers. We lost our shoes and took off our socks and met other children and ran with them. I remember my mother and father holding hands and for a few hours on a Sunday in may we were a family and we were happy."

Again no one spoke, Ray drank a lot more beers, we all did even Pam who had been freaked out by Ray patted him on the shoulder as she went for another beer.

In the morning. I woke up with a painful bear hangover and smiled, the familiar feeling of the hangover that I had have had hundreds of times, was the one normal thing in a long time. Ray had made us some breakfast and as I looked at him all the normal from a few seconds ago went out the widow. Here was what could have been a spawn of hell setting out a nice breakfast of eggs, ham orange juice, yogurt butter toast and what smelt like some hazelnut coffee while waring his nice little kitchen apron. We all sat down holding out heads and he started talking.

"Each one of you have a tracking device implanted in you, in your feet, down here they don't work, to much interference but as soon as you get back up there they can pull up your location on any device. So after breakfast I think you should try to get them out of you."

I took a sip of the coffee, it was delicious. "You mean cut them out of our feet?"

"Grow up, yes cut them out." Julie Julie Julie

In a couple of hours the four of us were hoping on one foot and following Ray into another the room.

"You guys are going to need new clothes."

He had horded up quite a lot of stuff, we all looked around for something in the warehouse store pile. I found a nice little mid-length pea coat and some easy fitting jeans.

Pam put a put on a linen flower dress with a little fake yellow flower in her hair and sandals, but god bless her the hippie look was offset by her ever present contrast, one of the things that made her so interesting. . So the almost see through love child dress was offset by the black bustier under it and her little flower of love was almost dangerous looking when you say the tube of the high powered smart rifle she had strung over her shoulder in the background.

Julie went with a simple white shirt and jeans with some margarita beads, which made her d cups look even bigger. She kept all the originally guns, said it didn't make a difference to here and I believed her.

"Where did you get all this stuff?"

"For awhile I felt that dressing was the only freedom I had so I started stealing from the trucks and you never know what's in the box until you open it."

"And the guns?" Pam loved here rifle and it looked good on her.

"They have a guy that watches me 24hours a day, once in a while it's one that so green I can pick him off, or sometimes they shit on themselves drop everything and run as soon as they see me. So I pick up there guns and something I get lucky and the police leave a van for me to pick late at night.

"Why haven't you ever tried to make a run for it?" Julie always so practical.

One time I took the guy out and made a run for it, made it all the way to 50th street before I met the team. You see the guy that is watching is not suppose to stop me, just keep an eye on me for the team. There not military, well not exclusively, they came out of an experiment from 2009, during the middle of the Iraqi war.

The government would take two guys from prison two from the CIA secret army, two family guys that had huge debts and one straight military trainer. They still don't know why but this particular combination produces something beautifully evil. These guys would go through fucking everything. Since then they have had thousand of upgrades, thousand of different mixes. I can tell you if one of these teams if after you, you are not getting out."

"And you're telling us this why?" I already knew

"Because if you're thinking of leaving the game, one of those teams will be after you."

"Do they have a name" Pam like names, she believes everyone and everything name has both the key to there happiness and key to there defeat.

"Name, no name, do you put a name on the knife that is stuck in your back when you sleeping?"

"So is there a way to get away?" Ben still didn't trust our new friend Bob.

"Well, an idea, really not a plan." He had his weird smile on his face, with the horns it was creepy."

"First have you ever heard of Red Ray?"

Julie took it "Of course Red Ray. used in every single device on the globe, it's basic function programming is being taught as early as third grade."

Yes, as early as third grade" Again the creepy smile.

"Red Ray was originally a series of games administered to most violent criminals in outsourced or provide prisons. They found that the languages somehow made its way its way into the subconscious and made the subjects more reasonable, more logical in their thinking. The major benefit to the prison was that violence did slow down, it stopped.

The subjects where simply not interested in violence and could in fact see no reason for it.

The pentagon got a whiff of this and tried an experiment in Candom New Jersey, which at the time was one of the most violent, cites in the USA. They added a small running line under every advertising bill board and outside in town running simple words using the language, these targeted advertising ran under every commercial every mental link everywhere all the time.. Violence stopped in three months and more than that, industry and art all exploded in this little NJ town. "

"Mother fuckers."

"They found only two flaws, the first was if the subject was away from the language for more than a week, the mind would return to it's normal status. The second was the more the mind was exposed to the language, the less emotions the subject seems to have. The mind so completely organized around logic. Anyway the pentagon dropped the project because one of those passions that apparently couldn't survive in the new mind was and intense loyalty. Something that is needed when you are asked to run to a place where you will most likely be shot to bits"

Julie finished it for him "However, the UN found the language useful in its project to standardize the communications interfaces of small to mid size devices worldwide. I also guess is the reason the pentagon is the only major player in the world that doesn't use the Red Ray language."

"Yes, even the new nameless teams that work for unknown entities uses it, makes the agents easier to manage, but also points to a weakness."

"Well" Ben again.

"Well I think the only chance you have of beating the team is to do something that no one else has done, something illogical, you should go after them."

"What?"

"Each one of this team, thinks like a little computer, each one has already plotted out all the logical probabilities of your actions again that is all the logical probabilities."

"Magic?" we all looked at Pam.

"Magic, myth, underworld, fear, we need to make them believe in these things, we need to make them believe that there is more to the world then logic, we must make them believe in the unknown."

"Yes, anyone for a drink" Pam, how many times have I heard you say those words, when will release the rope and let your fall into the black hole of your own making?

We sat down again and started drinking, it was hard to tell time down here but Ray told us it was about 3:00pm. We planed all day and most of the night, taking a break once and awhile to eat. We decided that the best moment to move would be 12:00am, that time in the middle of darkness and light that time when the two world touch. That time that in every culture is marked as the time of the unknown. So we started walking down the tunnel at about 11:30pm. I believe, like everyone that this was the last walk we were ever going to take so I and everyone else was really drunk.

At 12:00am Ben shot a "door knocker" up to the grate that separated up from the real world. The knocker was really just a 3 foot pipe that fit over the shotgun and had a square on the other side, army used them to knock down doors from a distance, it sent the grate spinning in the air about 50 feet. The boom almost shattered my ear drums and could image everyone up top stopping in there tracks, I hop no one was standing on that grate. Julie Pam and me git the hole with 5 smoke shells each , nothing toxic, just cover. more. Ray told us the grate exited out to one of those ridiculous park bench and 5 trees that they call a park NYC, the smoke should be pretty much up to the tree tops.

Ray turned off the electrical for about 5 blocks around, but he made them flicker a little first for affect, then we waited to let them get used to it. Then Ben fired three high powered flash shells, to blind the boys with the night vision, flowed by my favorite a small EMP shell, without all their tech they we just folks. They we headed up the ladder and out as fast as we could. Each heading for a target except for Ray and Pam,

Pam was too drunk to do much she had kind of channeled the oracle at Delhi, she said Ray and her should stay in the center of the smoke and dance. When she first said it we just laughed but she was serious and arguing with a drunken person is like tits on a bull. There was a constant beat that was reverberating throughout the walls of the building, you couldn't make out what the music was, just the beat., coming from uptown.

Pam took off her clothes but not here shoes, she hates to get he feet dirty and Ray stripped to revel that his dick was proportion to his huge body. So the woman danced with a demon under sick malnourished trees in NYC as the smoke swirled and slowly dissipated around them.

I could feel, we all could, the men stationed all around the area, waiting for us now transfixed by this impossible display. Nothing in there little tidy minds, with there linear progression and probabilities could process the images before them. I could feel them transfixed, all trying to analyze.

My man was on the roof of the building to the left of the park, he heard me open the door to the roof, but he couldn't turn around fast enough I got him with a shot in the chest. That was just to knock the wind out of him since he had a vest on, I keep running to him firing and one shot grazed his ear and the other one finally got him in the nose. I looked over and saw Pam and Ray dancing and understood why she said we needed to do it. Then I saw a window across the park light up again and again, there was a pause then it started again..

Shots started raining down on Pam and Ray but they kept dancing and somehow the bullets weren't getting to them, maybe Pam's idea of getting real spirit help wasn't all that crazy. Three men came at them firing then Julie came out of some void and fired a net shell at them when they were trapped the net electrified them, not like a Tazer, this net turned there brains into a hot smoking Jello substance.

All the men were dead or hiding and I joined Pam and Ray dancing then Julie and Ben joined . We were still drunk and the exasctyof having lived and being able to live one more day was better than anything I ever put in my mouth. Ben fired 3 more smoke shells and we ran uptown, adding to our mystery and madness for those logic brains, if there were any still watching us. We ran flat out for about five blocks and scrambled into a hallway of a brownstone. There we all throw up and cried and gnashed our teeth, except for Ray.

"Now they will be afraid of you." Ray was not as drunk as the rest of us, much bigger body I guess

"Hey Ben, could you stop looking at my wife's tits."

"What? Oh yeah"

"Honey, are you sober enough to put you cloths on?" her answer was to fall down on the floor.

"Ray, could you do me a favor and knock on that door there."

Ray knocked at the door of apartment IC a man opened the door and looked right at Ray's huge crank and smiled, then looked up saw his horns and ran. I dragged Pam into the apartment and the rest followed.

"Hey Ray put some cloths on"

"No hurry," Julie was looking right at me and smiling.

I dress Pam on the couch and Julie took the chair next to her, Ray came out dressed in leather pants and sneakers and slept on the floor.

Ben and I went to the kitchen to scrounge and talk.

"So Ben, how many time's did you shoot the guy?"

"I stopped counting at 20, really after that I was more like splatter painting. How about you?"

"Only three you know how I'm a cheap bastard."

"You know I love Pam like a sister but she's crazy."

"Yeah I know and I hope you don't look at your sisters tits like that."

"So where to now?"

"Well I think we are about 38th street which puts us close the The church of ass."

The church of the ass whose real name is The Church of the Chou Wang was created by the Davos group and is worldwide. One of their geniuses decided to consolidate all the strip clubs, whore houses and independent hookers in the world by making them a religious group run by the local states.

Every city in the world had at least one sites all standardized. 11 strippers polls of pure gold and engraved with snakes and dragons These projected out of a round stage that was covered in purples velvet. The stage also had crystal cock statutes of all kinds, some human, some animal and even some since fictions ones. Like the octopus with a man's face . on the end of every tentacle was a cock which some would ride as part of there bit.

Naked woman and men danced 24hours a day rain or shine, in the burring heat of NYC August and the subzero of February in Moscow.. They have special events that are designed to undermined the worlds existing religious, like the Christmas orgy, or the month of food sex during Ramada.

Little porno goldmines, one third would go to the local government and the rest would go to the group Of course now, only the church was allowed to have strippers and porno and all the other forms of flesh pedaling that used to be part of the world. Even the little videos that kids download onto there mind phones whee stamped CCW. At each site there was always at least 2000 people at any site and here in NYC it was closer to10,000 on a slow day, All filmed and pumped out on network, cable and the Internet live from 42$^{nd}$ and time square.

"We can use them as cover for about 20 blocks; I don't think anyone wants what's going on here going worldwide."

"Yeah your right."

So new plan?" Pam was dressed and ready to go, the Jekyll Hyde thing always went with day and night.

"Well nothing fancy, we run right through the ass church. The idea is that who ever is running this thing won't want that kind of coverage."

"When?"

"Now."

Lust and greed are more gullible then innocence.

*Mason Cooly*

The whole room full of monitors and men and woman from all over the world, all frozen, every mouth open. They all had seen something that had never happened, one of the Davos teams had been destroyed, killed off like regular street cops. But Peter wasn't shocked he was staring intently at the eyes of the two couples. He saw something, something he and his group had been searching for something he couldn't write, talk about or even think about.

"We need all the video feeds to that incident destroyed." red shirts, not one thought about the guys that just got killed. I would never work for those bastards.

"Good luck with that, this is NYC the chances if you getting every video before it hits the Internet are pretty slim."

Sam walks out of the room and back to his office, he reached out to his own team and tells them to stand down, but he really didn't know why. He just had this feeling, a feeling that these two couples were going to do a lot more then make it to the bridge and he just wanted to see it play out. While he was standing there he felt a smile come over his face, he couldn't remember the last time he smiled.

"Jamal and Chiquia met 3 years ago, at party, both where B and E specialist. They hit it off right away, were married a year later and ran one of the must prolific B and E crews in NJ. Both having a tech background, they were able to bypass the increasingly complex home surcuity systems coming out. In a lot of ways the new home systems made the house, alive in it's own right with a distinct self preservation instinct.

Once the cops came to their modest ranch house in union NJ while they were having a barbq with friends on a really beautiful July Day. The cops were rookies and thought they could get on the fast track by nabbing some elephants. So they came to their house and tried to strong arm them in front of their friends and family.

They never forgot it, when the cops and their families went to mid- night mass on Christmas Jamal and Chiquia stole everything thing in their house down to the ornaments on their Christmas tree, they did the same thing to mothers, brothers and sisters. For new years they sent the police precinct a sex video of one of the cops wife with her lover. And sent another cop a tape of his daughter giving head to 3 guys for drugs right in their kitchen.. No one ever bother them again.

They knew the streets and knew sometimes the easiest way to win is to eliminate the competition and to them this game was not different. So they are waiting across the street of a Mega Wal-Mart in the village. Finally a couple came out with new clothes on that they changed into in the store. They stared holding hands and looked happy, like the new clothes gave them a new start. Jamal and Sniqua starting firing at them with the both hands, Jamal going with the one after the other, Sniqua firing both at the same time. They empty all four clips into them, then went over to make sure they dead, they where and about ten people that were around the couple when the shooting started.

I

It was time to run again

"OK RUN"

Our new friend Ray wanted to take the lead, the way he explained it he was going to die no matter what, he wanted his last moments of life to mean something. As soon we hit the street I could clearly make out the music from the church of the ass, they had a new song every month and thanks to their contacts no matter how bad the song was it always made it to the top of the charts. This months lyrics were, as always inspiring to the followers.

"Why don't you get me drunk and fuck me up the ass."

Beat, Beat, Beat, Beat

"I don't want to think or make any plans."

Beat beat beat, BEAT

"Pour it down my mouth, Stick it between my cheeks."

Beat beat beat, beat

"I'm so drunk, got two more holes for you friends Sam and Pete."

Beat beat beat beat

We he the outside of the crowd with Ray pushing them out of the way. The ass church had plenty of bounces, not to stop guys from touching the woman but for guys who wouldn't pay. They used high powered tazers, Phase sticks and were trained in new Yoshikan Akido, but they didn't slow Ray down at all. We made it to the stage in about 15mins; Ben froze as he looked up, 11 women had the head dress burka on and where performing sex on men they had taken from the audience and the pigs and cows of crystal on stage. I tried to call him but with the blasting music and the screams of the crowd you couldn't hear anything. Then a woman from the crowd grabbed him and started stoking his dick, which got her a pistol whip from Julie and woke Ben up. Making it around the stage was much harder, the crowd was dense and there where clumps of people fucking right there on the street.

It took us another 15 mins to get to the other side of the stage and start going back up town. That's when I heard them, well really felt them,Custs. the whole crowd felt them that strange vibration of the air that can only be caused by the odd wings ,every one stopped doing whatever they were doing. Then the DJ turned the music off and we all hear the unmistakable whirling of Custs.

After the war with Mexico, a lot of Americans wanted to drop nukes on Mexico. Most wanted every single Mexican out of the country and to close the border. The generals told the new American president that not making a retaliatory strike was really not an option. The problem was this was the first time that war had come to American soil in hundreds of years and the American people just wanted to go back to their lives, to forget. The Air force had a solution and the state department saw and opportunity.

Wayne Brendan delivered his now famous "Fifth trumpet" speech in the destroyed downtown Los Angles. Ninety percent of the speech was about how America would rebuild, become stronger endure. How it's people still had that pioneer spirit. But the speech is remembered for the last lines.

"And should our enemies having lost their quest for conquest now be free to return to their homes and families after shedding the blood of so many innocent Americans, Should I turn my face away from the fires of American cites that even now block out the sun and poison the air. I say no, America says no and god said no."

"Let the words of the holy bible be there epitaph.

Rev 9:1 And the fifth angel sounded, and I saw a star fall from heaven unto the earth: and to him was given the key of the bottomless pit. Rev 9:2 And he opened the bottomless pit; and there arose a smoke out of the pit, as the smoke of a great furnace; and the sun and the air were darkened by reason of the smoke of the pit. Rev 9:3 And there came out of the smoke locusts upon the earth: and unto them was given power, as the scorpions of the earth have power.

And he walked away from the cameras.

Three years before the pentagon had finished is most advance and easy to build no manned aircraft. A simple device the size of small fridge and shaped like a pill, with two propellers, two m230 30-mm automatic canon's mounted on either side an on z series hellfire missiles. It cost them about 5000us per for each not including the cannon's admissible, which where stockpiled anyway for the apache helicopters, the made 1,million of them and let each and everyone of them lose on Mexico city.

The CIA had extracted every single bit of data from the Mexican governments database during the war. A database that included the rip number of every man woman and child in Mexico city born in the last 30 years. As part of a treaty with the US, all Mexicans born had a been implanted with a locater so they would know if they crossed the border each with it's own rip code that could be brought up in real time on any Internet attached device. So the pentagon just loaded the numbers into there drones and sent them off to seek and destroy. The world watched live as every man woman and child in Mexico city was hunted down and killed. After which America toke control of the Mexican government

"Until such time that these institutions could be rebuilt for the good of the people."

The whole world knew the sound of custs all feared it and now here in NYC we all heard that sound and for a few seconds no one moved. Then one came around a building and all began to run like one living organism. I ran with everyone else but I wasn't afraid, I knew we where going to die.

I dated a girl in collage named Lisa Rodriquez, I used to call her a computer geek, she would always correct me with "I a network nerd". One day while downing lots of rum and smoking some buda I asked what the difference was. She told me computer geeks write code, some interesting some not but most are stagnate, dead, meant for one purpose, maybe it's to balance a checkbook or play a game or run a robot that cleans floors. Whatever the program is it has a beginning middle and end. The network is alive, always changing, developing, improving, more like a human mind than anything else, each node making connections to other nodes, which makes connections to others just like the human mind.

She wrote her theses on the custs, they where made with very limited programming, fly, find, kill, evade attack. But their networking capability with really unlimited and it's that networking that made them more deadly than any nuclear device. In Mexico City the network made one huge killing mind and that mind reached out to laptops, traffic cams, core computers, cell phones, and car computers. It became a god of death, able to see, everywhere at once.

So as they mowed down whole families with there cannons, there we also causing cars to crash, cell phone batteries to explode, electrical systems to overload and set buildings on fire. Everywhere the network was it was being used to kill and the more it killed the better it got at it, pushing probabilities to the extreme.

She talked about one of the custs that had it's weapon locked on a family in a little. camery coming right at it at about 90 miles an hour. The 30 millimeter cannon would make the car and the people into a meat and blood pulp. But it didn't, it shot its wheel, which made the car go out of control and go right into natural gas pipe that was in front of an apartment building. Killing the family in the car and everyone in the building. The network could see everything in Mexico City at once, it could plot it's the future and change the future to one where more people died.

As we ran I saw three people who were so drugged out they were still fucking while everyone was running, fucking until one of the cannons locked on them and they vanished. That is the thing that is the hardest to get your mind around, the 30mill cannons don't kill people they destroy them, like taking a hammer to an ant, and soon there is nothing that even looks like an ant.

I keep running following Ben who looked like he was running somewhere. We were against a building now and we could see the custs coming our way, mowing down everyone in front of them. There were only five of them, but more than enough for us. I looked over and saw Ben screaming but I couldn't hear a thing above the screaming of the crowd. Ray was crying, he bent down and gave Pam a kiss and opened his huge hand to show her the trackers that where in our feet, I don't know when he removed them or why we didn't feel it.. The he ran, fast, faster than any human could and the custs followed him.

As soon as they went after him we starting running as fast as we could over the bits of body's, running blood and derbies. Then one broke off and came after us, seems they had developed a deep distrust of humans, can't say I blame them. There it is, the cannon locked on us, inevitable. Building windows exploded thousands and thousands of bullets hit the cust, it tried to turn to fight but still more bullets hit it and now some rockets. Ben yanked my hand and we ran again and the fear came back all at once, drying my through, chocking off my breath, because now I thought we had a chance, a little chance to live.

"Look" Pam pointed down the street and one of the cysts was lying there with a million holes in it and right next to it was Ray. His body was mostly gone but his head was still in one piece. The horns out of place with the now on such a restful face.

Pam knelt down and very gently touched Rays face, then she took out a knife and cut one off his horns and put it in here back pack.

"Guys, we should keep running" They all turned to look at me and I could hear "what and ass hole" coming out of their eyes, but we started running again.

There was a a lot of dead and we the living ran past them, not sure if where putting distance between us and terabytes of networked connected death or heading right to our own personal waterloo. I started to look at the people and the parts of people on the sidewalk. Ben looked at the mess and turned his head sideways like my dog brandy used when she saw something she didn't understand.

If you looked at New York from space parts of it would looked like a maze with millions people trying to find their way out. If you in the maze on any given block there are building 50 stories or higher on both side, so really you are standing huge ravine with only one way in and one way out.

The custs in Mexico City, whose buildings were many times the size of some of the old buildings in NY, found that it was more effective to drop the building on the people running in the man made valleys. They would use there cannons to hit the top floors of the buildings. Making it rain glass, brick, concrete and steel, all falling on people from from 20 stories up.. Most where sliced in half by the glass, some pulverized by the falling concrete, thousands could be killed in one block. I looked north and saw one of the custs shooting at the building, and then south the same, I knew from my history one more was somewhere above us and would just start shooting into us randomly. We could die from the bullets or run into the building falling and get crushed to death, there was really no way out.

"What the fuck are we going to do?"

Ben and the rest of them didn't know there was really nothing to do, nothing except pick which way to go, I had already decided, I just loaded up my clips and started looking up for the one that would come in on us. Any just like millions of years ago when the single cells for reasons we will never know started to work together and become one organism. So now the 4 of us spread out without works, without electrical pulses without pheromones we are one.

Here it comes arching over the cust from the north and coming straight down into the street the canon rotating faster and faster as the bullets fire up the street, cars are ripped in half. The side walk gyrates from the impact of the metal. I am standing in the center of the street looking right up and firing up my 9mm, waiting for death wondering if I will feel pain when the 30mills turn me into little pieces of chop meant. Out of the corner of my eye I see Ben and the rest of my body that is not my body, and that's when it finally understand family.

He shoot a net at the thing and it starts to bang up against the building it's propellers slowing down, getting caught in the metal net. It's still shooting at us it will contuie to shoot until it's out. Ben starts shooting carbonize Vulcan tips at it, like little flying acetylene torches burning through it. I could feel myself smiling, imaging that I, of all the millions of humans that have walked barefoot, sandaled and sneakered across this planet and others, that I and only I will destroy death. That I will lift up that stupid back robe and fuck the puss laden asshole, I feel joy as I pump bullets into the control center of the custs. This is for Michelangelo, for Einstein, for that 6 year old girl Carmen who lived across the street from me and use to ware pink dresses and blow the dandelions and you ran over her with a car. It was lying in the street and the rest of my new extended body was pulling me away from it I just kept firing, spiting, cursing at it. We life, fucker, we live.

They slammed me up against the building were we all waited for the beautiful twin waterfalls of crushing bones and flesh to reach us. I could hear Ben screaming as always he sounded very far away against the thundering sound of falling buildings. Even with all that I could tell he was scared. I was still smiling, I had chain sawed the arms of Shiva, put c4 in that feces smelling ferry on the river Styx. Then just like in the movies I started to see my life pass before my eyes as small parts of debris started to reach us. It was strange; I was expecting the fuzzy montage of my life, my first girlfriend, puppy, tab of acid.

What I was seeing was my brother out of a in the window of a startbucks across the street, I guess every one flashback is different. He started waving at me and yelling, but I couldn't hear him, I knew he wanted me to come, I thought for a second that I must be going to hell if he was in a starbucks then I wondered when he died and that the guys that came to get us on my wedding night may have got to him. I started walking to him, moving away from my little group that had insisted on firing at the custs until the end. They all ran up behind me pushing me in to the store with my brother.

I guess everyone's hell was different and mine is a starbucks, makes sense I will always be around people but never close to them. My brother is there, staring at me with at same face and big eyes; I use to laugh at when he was in the crib.

"Joe, when did you die?" I needed to know.

"Die? He through same water in my face.

"Wake up time, we need to get out of here."

Consciousness came back to me and I heard everyone laughing at me.

"You know when victor was a kid he lived in California for a while and spent a whole month on blotter acid. He still gets flashbacks."

Everyone reacts to stress in a different way, in that way it is a lot like love. I heard war stories with guys in a firefight stopping to masturbate and some just nodding off to sleep and some look like they are working just fine but they don't remember anything. That was me, as I'm sitting on some bed in someone's apartment my hands start shaking then the rest of my body as everything starts coming back to me. Pam holds me close and the rest of the group leaves the room, then the hugs turn to kisses and I remember that we never did have a wedding night.

When you love someone sometimes you make love and sometimes you fuck, this time was the later. I woke up and Pam was taking some alcodios which you can get on any street corner. It gives you the same high you get with liquor but can put them in your pocket and they don't register on the Breathalyzer. Most people buy a beer and put two or three of the pills in, makes a hell of a drink. No hangover, no liver damage, no puking.. just get as drunk as you want legally and still rise and shine in time for work the next day.

I went to the living room and everyone was asleep except for Joe, who was on guard at the window. Mu brother had been an army ranger which made me feel a whole lot better that we had someone with some real military experience and someone I could trust.

"So, how do you like NY?" Joe hated NY, hated all cities since he did most of his time in Argentina, going building to building, he saw any city as one big death trap.

"Don't give up your day job."

My day job, I hadn't thought about it, but I guess if we do make it out of NY, I'll be unemployed, nice.

"How did you know we were here and how did you find us?"

"I still have some contacts, and finding you wasn't very hard, I just followed the sirens until I found the right group." I always hated when he did that, secret government contacts, every time he didn't want to answer a question it was secret government contacts time.

"How long are you going to sing that same song?"

"This time I mean it. You want to hear the part that really freaked me out, they do this every year and every year there is a huge amount of shit that goes down in some city and no one covers it. Not on TV, not on the Internet I wasn't even able to get a decent street rumor on this, that's how buried this shit it."

"Well did your fiends' in dark undisclosed locations have a way to get us out of this?"

"I watched some video when they did this on Miami, half of the couples had joined forces and one of them had some pretty serious family connections with the Brazilian gangs. We are talking a small paramilitary army, with home court advantage, very hard going for any military group. They burned the whole neighborhood down to the ground and everyone that tried to get out didn't make it, not even pieces. The only way you're going to make it out of here is to get across that bridge; the couples that finish are the only ones that live."

"Great, hey speaking of couples, what the hell is wrong with them?"

Ben and Julie were on opposite sides of the living room like opposing magnets.

"Not sure, either your friend is a minute man and your five hour bout with Pam made them both feel uncomfortable or the woman wishes it was her making all that noise. By the way I didn't know Pam had the lungs for it."

"Dude."

"Sorry."

Inside I laughed because Pam was the type of woman that everyman would eventually wind up sleeping around on and be the one that never saw it coming. The type of woman that was to tired for sex after a long day and would tell you to wake her up in the morning, only to reject you 70 percent of the time then. The type that you actually had to explain to that sex with your partner is more important then clean dishes or American idol or her brothers girl friend losing her job for the fifth time. The type that you would eventually give up on trying to convince her. Not because I didn't like a quickie as much as the next man, but eventually you ask yourself what happened? What happened to the candles and lingerie and the sometimes tied to the bedpost and a good solid blow job and you decide those memories are precious and every time you have some of the appropriately scheduled non-sex, you are losing those memories just a little. It was the first real sex I had in two years.

"So secret agent man, how did you manage to stop that first cust?"

"Wasn't me, looks like someone else is looking after your group in a big way. I tried to help you out at 14th street, but that freak got to you anyway."

"Ray, his name was Ray." Pam, always the fighter of lost causes.

"OH, yeah sure."

"So, do you have any information that can help?" sounded like Julie was done with her brooding.

"I got nothing; I tried to find something, anything that could maybe lead to a guy, who knows a guy, to get us out of here. I got nothing, well maybe, something but its crazy." Julie started laughing,

"Crazy, how can it be anymore crazy then the shit we are already in. A couple a nights ago, I was sipping a martin in a way to tiny bikini just looking to get laid, which I didn't thanks to my husband mister softie. Today I was running with a mutant demon, across hundreds of half naked assholes while robotic refrigerator size locust shot at me with cannons.

So please, don't hold back on the crazy, believe me I'll fit right in with the rest of the day."

We were silent for a couple of seconds just looking at her without mouths open, except for Ben who was looking out the window.

"The ass hole of the devil."

"Come on Victor don't start with that shit again." I had head the story a million times.

They all insisted that victor tell them, if they knew him like I did they would know they wouldn't have to ask him to tell the story, they would have to ask him not to like I had a thousand times. I left the room to look for liquor and stumbled across the owners of the apartment tied up in one of the bedrooms and apologized like I walked in on them naked. I finally found a nice bottle of vodka in the freezer and sat in the kitchen drinking from the bottle, I can almost hear Victor in the other room telling the story or is it in my head from all the times I heard it.

The asshole of the devil was a fairy tale that Victor had picked up while he was in the army rangers serving in Africa and it's a good one. It starts with one of the kids, whose Parents were killed in 911, he became a building designer, after learning so much about the construction of the towers while still a kid.

Anyway the kid becomes one of the top ten architectures in the world and gets his dream come true, to work on a building in NYC,he got to build a school way uptown. It's all over the news links, home time kid makes good, rising from the ashes, fill in your own Yale/Harvard journalism punchy byline. Then the story gets crazy, seems the kid was not as well adjusted as people thought. The legend says in the school basement he build a tunnel, not just any tunnel a tunnel that could survive a nuke attack, a tunnel that had provisions for 777 people for 21 months, a tunnel that had a small arsenal with trucks and a little gas station. Like a survivalist wet dream right in New York City. But thats not the part that keeps the story alive, the part that keeps guys running around all the schools in Manhattan and combing research libraries at 3AM is the gold, 1492 pounds of gold American eagle coins are in the tunnel, if there is one.

The best part of the story, well for me being a netneron guy,was the postscript, this story had been going around for years, so thousands have looked for gold in the asshole until they used all their money and lives. But whoever this guys was, he knows how to cover his tracks. Not only can his name not be found in any of the records on any NYC data bases, but the names of everyone in his company where changed, so you didn't know who built what and when. Pictures of every school every superintendent, every police surveillance and traffic pictures of the schools gone, all phone records, gone, all bank transaction gone, they couldn't even find record of the kids lunch money.

The lines between the virtual world and the real world had blurred long ago, but there were still some rules from the wall was in place. An object has a weight on the virtual world just like objects in space, the more data on the object the greater is virtual mass. Public schools in NYC are like black holes, the virtual density incredibly massive literally millions of data streams are sucked into them. But then one day, , hundreds of black holes, in a virtual universe are replaced with flat space. Gone everything about them, every link, every blog, every single bit of data gone. The legend says that every a year later when you tired to add data about there schools anywhere, even in personal bio ROM in peoples head, it would disappear. Something that that armies all over the world are trying to replicate.

Ben comes into the kitchen grabs the vodka from my hand and takes a cup of and does a quick shot.

"Listen, your brother is about as useless as tits on a bull. First he tells us that we don't have a chance in hell then he tells us a long story about a way out but no one has ever found it. I just about to check to see if I have a special shot gun shell that shoots duck tape over people's mouths."

"Man, I couldn't use that for every girlfriend I ever had."

We both laughed and both kept drinking.

"So still no plan?"

"Nope, just keep running up town and hope we can handle whatever shit is going to come our way.

Julie came in and joined us in the kitchen which is a NY city is smaller then a porta poti so it was really tight with three people., she took two shots.

"Hey, Vic you want to hear something funny?"

"Oh yeah, please do some stand up."

"Asshole. Anyway, I think I know the old man that your brother is talking about." I love the way wife's can walk into a room and not talk to you.

"What old man"

"It was at the end of the story but you didn't stay to finish it like you never finish anything you do."

Oh now she is talking to him

"He said no one has ever found the tunnel, or even the school the tunnel might be in, or anybody that worked with the Kid on the project except for one. They say the kid had one helper about the same age as him, an Indian designer that was blind." God please make me stop looking at her tits.

"I use to spend some weekends with my cousin Frances in the city up by the highland park in Dominican town. Turns out she had a $7^{th}$ grade Indian math teacher who was blind",

"There has to be a duck tape in here"

She looked mad, really mad so I thought I would just ask some questions and see where it goes.

"When was the last time you saw this guy?' At that Ben stormed out.

"I don't know, 15 maybe 20 years ago." She got it on that one question, nothing in this city stays in place very long, it was more like a living thing then any one wanted to admit.

"Fuck, well its right next to the bridge so if we get that close I'm checking it out, by myself if I have to."

"So we run then?"

"Yeah."

"Got them sir" Employee number 937802

"Let me see, yes. Where?"

"$34^{th}$ st"

"Get some locals to watch the street send a Davos squad there and make sure not one gets out."

Employee number 937802 keep watching, in 2025 cable companies added a built in web cam cable box, with a speaker phone so you could video teleconference right on you TV by just dialing the phone number you wanted to connect to on you remote. Since then there has been one installed every every type of electronic device, from dishwasher to pool pump, so you can connect with engineers or support in real time for trouble shooting. Off course, with camera and phones installed in everywhere, they could watch you also. Illegal feeds of all kinds from people home were bought and sold on the every day since then.. And every day, just like today the government found someone that didn't want to be found.

They five of them started running up town and came to a crowed NYC corner, redundant because every corner in NYC is crowed.

"Stop." Joe still had that army voice and when he said stop, people stopped.

"What time for another fairy tale, something about the asshole that tells stories that are meaningless until his friend's beats the shit out of him?"

"Something wrong." He was looking around but couldn't 'place it first, then he saw them, links.

Links were another attempted at elevating the human mind without genetic engineering, the theory was simple. Link a lot of brains together and they could all share knowledge and the whole would become greater then the parts. Turned out to have just the opposite effect, as not only information but emotions were shared the least common denominator won. Like a committee, the one that had the most fear determined how much risk they would take, the one with the most will determined all there paths. They all became a part of one person not a fusion of many.

The Brazilian army came up with a version they used in combat, one strong leader with twenty bodies. In the prototypes some of the leaders would go crazy, the feeling of godhood too much for them as they could see and be and fuck in twenty places at once. But after a while it was the a perfect soldier with twenty bodies, like having a hundred arms and legs. They only way you could tell them apart was in a crowd with normal people, the bodies, had no real will of there own, so they would have to fake, doing normal things and they were terrible at it. Sometimes they would just do the same thing over and over again, like that woman in the nice dress who keeps dialing her cell phone and bringing it to her ear, over and over again. Just like that other woman in the nice blue jeans and rocker leather jacket.

"What?" I waited for Joe since he was the only one with real combat experience, well I guess I should say the most combat experience now.

"Links, an all woman cell, never seen one before" Joe was scanning the crowd because once you spotted one you could spot the whole group, it's something you only have to see once. Twenty people with the same exact body language, even seeing two makes the hairs on your arm stand up. The hunter way in the back of your brain sends a scream that makes it through years of conditioned reason; you feel something is very wrong.

"You guys want to tell us what the fuck is going on?" Ben never liked to be in the dark, you know the type ask you were we are going 5 times in the car.

"No time, Joe taking the straight line?" If Joe was right we had to hurry, I was hoping my little group would take me on faith.

"Yeah, I hate you."

"Julie, Pam, look for a woman that has blue jeans and a leather jacket, her makeup will set her apart from average woman on the street, more aggressive. When you find her kill her." They looked at me and I nodded and they took off, man I hope I just didn't give the OK to kill some innocent woman.

"Ben follow us and do what we do."

The power of the links is also there weakness, the link makes them one person, which is way there are some dance shows on Broadway with them, the one mind making a beautiful dance of many bodies moving as one. But they also share their feelings and even though they train the leading link to control it, it you catch that on by surprise, the rest are useless. Joe slide right behind the woman with the cell phone and shot her in the back of the head. The crowd panicked except for 18 woman who just squatted a little and pulled out the exact same gun.

I got one shot off in the chest one of them before the crowd started pushing me all over the place. The rest of the woman started shooting at us, Joe got two right away, all that army training, Ben blew a hole in one the size of a dinner plate, then Joe got another one shooting right thought that hole. I was being pushed back into 30 rock by about three of them, even then my mind was still freaking about how they moved, they had me pined and where coming in, I had maybe 2 mins. I kept peeking out returning fire, but they were still coming. . I put my hand out again to get a couple more shots off but all I got where two very loud and terrifying clicks, clicks that left me so stunned that my mouth opened into a huge O.

Two tiny hands with nice painted pink fingernails grabbed my forearm and yanked me into the sky, I looked back as I was flying and saw two rocker woman running after my flying body and the big statue of Prometheus laughing at me. I hit the street in a slide, the skin of my forearms pulled back like a plum's blood oozing out. I tried to get up as fast as I could but a foot got me on my right side and another on the left side of my head.

I have been beat up a lot when I was a kid, long time ago, back when people aged and died all the time, I lived in a Puerto Rican section in the Bronx but dated this Irish girl. Sometimes I didn't make it back home without a reminder that I should not be in their part of town, so I knew the first thing to go when your body is being beaten and shaken up is reason and logic, I had to find a way to buy me a couple of seconds to regroup. They did me a favor and kicked me again sent me rolling down the street and I get up and ran, well more like a hobble, but it gave me two minutes, even with the sound of the perfectly instep feet chasing me, I was able to think. I thought it would be a help, but with a few mins of clarity, it just became that much clearer that I was screwed. My hand to hand fighting was almost good but these two where like CIA fighters. On top of that I knew that the links could select one of the group to feel all the pain so the others might not feel pain at all.

I turned around and they were coming right at me, in the little space between them I could see Ben up against a wall getting hammered, but Ben is so big and these woman so small it would have looked funny except for the blood coming out of his face. I waited until they got close and pulled out my other 9mm which was also empty and hit one of them over the head with it. It cracked her head open, but she kept coming and the other one looked like she was mad, if they got mad. Slapped me in the face and kicked me in the knee, I went down face first, the bloody one sat on my back. She took put some chain around my neck and started to pull, man this was going to be a shitty way to go. As my back arched and my hands tried to get the chain around my neck, making gurgling pleads for her to stop which sounded a lot like something trying to sing while throwing up, the other one started to kick me in the face again and again again again.

I always thought the descriptions of death, as a person, over the centuries were completely wrong. Black robed and silent, or suited and eloquent it always made it seem like death was a reasonable fellow just doing his job. Those of us that have come close to death before knew different, death is nothing more than that high school bully roaming the hallways looking for victims. I could feel him now pushing me against the lockers, laughing, shaking me up and knocking my books out of my hands.

Then I started to hear my breathing again and feel my body, the warm blood dripping down my face, my throat full off flem trying to clear itself all the pain felt like an old friend now. The ladies had decided not to kill me, I think they made a very good choice and that fucking asshole death can wait a few more years. Then I started to hear the sound of water from the fountains decorated by brass animals and the wind across the globe that atlas holds on his shoulders. I looked up and there was Pam smiling down at me.

"Pam?"

"There was a woman sitting in the rainbow room all by herself having champagne and chocolate with a leather jacket and hooker red lipstick. The whole look was wrong for the rainbow room, I mean, it's like putting on a ball dress to go to a biker bar is was just wrong, so I shot her five times in the head." I always forget how tribal woman's make up is.

"Well Vic, looks like I may have been wrong when I said the woman was useless."They helped me up and I saw the links all around me on the ground, all in the fetal position crying with nothing on but underwear, pretty lacy underwear, I just kept staring at it.

"Honey, looking at crazy dead woman's asses is weird even by your standards." The only time Pam called me honey was when she was mad.

"Why are they naked?" I couldn't look away, it was like watching a stand up comic bomb in front of a huge crowd.

"Seems as soon as their main brain was dead they all went crazy, ripping off their clothes ,screaming, pucking pissing. Your type of woman" Juiles not to Veiled reference to Pam did not go unnoticed.

"Their underwear, they have on different ones, not all the same." I was mumbling to myself.

Somewhere deep inside of mind there was something left, something left of the Individuals, this was their only expression of a personality totally subjected. The underwear was the only thing that was truly their own, they had even written on them, little notes, like a diary.

"I think we better get him and us out of this very exposed spot and get some ammo." Ah Julie always thinking.

Yet another apartment, this time it was two girls, collage roommates, that has just done some Ecstasy and thought that being help at gunpoint, even without bullets with so sexy. My brother Joe helped himself and me and Ben sat at the window pretending not to listen to the humping by looking for food.

"Well without any ammo we are so screwed." As soon as he said it we all laughed and Julie and Pam did too, man one of those collage girls sounded like a monkey.

Pam found some liquor of course, which helped with deadening the sound and the pain from my very swollen face.

We fell asleep in the living room, drunk as skunks.

**You wish your dad had been there but more oftentimes he was not, you can't put your arms around a dirty gang-bang cum shot, but that's all you get. that's all you get."**

*Sara Silverman the porno song*

I woke up in pain, the next day is always worse, Julie told me my nose wasn't broken but she thought it really should be, she made one of her jokes about it. Said she hoped my cock was as hard as my nose, I said twice as hard, but only in a really tight pussy, then Pam came back in and all the fun left the room. I loved Pam but her endless depression just made life long and lifeless, at least when she was drunk she was mad, which was something I guess.

"So, gang I think I can get us some ammo." Joe was in a great mood, sleeping with two woman will do that to a man.

"Wait don't tell me, in the back of a magic dresser, all we have to do is ask the elf and follow the ring of power." Julie was wasting her time, my brother Joe hated movies and books.

91

"I know a guy on 63$^{rd}$ he's a dingo, but got out of porno ten years ago."

Pam and Julie made the universal gross sound that all woman make, you either loved dingo's or you hated them there was no middle ground. They started out as homeless kids on the streets of Brazil. When the rich European woman got tired of being molested by the Muslims in there own countries they stared heading to Brazil. There they would pick up the kids from the streets and use them as boy toys for a few euros'. Then one got the idea to modify them, surgically at first then genetically. Dingo's had thee dicks, one under the tough the one most men have and one like a tail off the coxes bone. That way the dingo could fill every hole of a woman at once. I heard stories that some woman killed themselves with dingo's, I guess not a bad way to go. Anyway, they took over the porn world, first as freaks then as the standard, now they run the show. There is no such thing as a poor dingo.

We didn't have any options so we waited until midnight, more so Joe could say a proper good bye to his new friends because with all of cover of darkness was pretty useless in a city that never sleeps. NYC never really got dark, I bet you could see some of the lights here from another dimension.

A teenage girl, maybe 16 open the door to his brownstone, young girls sought out dingo's, they where the holy grail of orgasms. Once they found one, they had to be thrown out and most times killed them self's afterward. I met a woman who said, she was in love and she had been with a dingo, the dingo was better.

"Joe, how the hell are you."?

The pricks, retract just like normal ones so he looked just like a normal middle aged Brazilian millionaire.

"You know Fabio, I'm short ammo and money same as normal."

"What, not horny, you getting old?"

"Who are your friends, wait, no, how could you bring them to my house?"

Dingo's knew everything on the street, in any given town the best source of information on the streets is you friendly neighborhood hooker. She knows everything because she experiences the street up close and personal and right between her legs. Hookers have more secrets told to them then any confessional. On top of that they had connections to everyone and everything.

"Hey there not serial killers" that is the best thing Joe could say about us.

"I wish they were, then you would only have local cops who didn't finish 6th grade looking for you in every bar and strip joint. Your little friends here are wanted by people so high up if they have a wet dreams someone is assigned make them real."

"Hey all we want is ammo."

"Joe, doesn't matter, as soon as you leave, we have to go, they know where you are and probably know where you are going. So you can come in take ammo and food and whatever else you need, But Joe, never show your face at my door again.". "

I could tell the porno guy was serious and knew the only reason we were here was because Joe had no choice. Right then I saw one of his girls eyes digging into us, a pure uncluttered hatred shinning from her eyes, like a mother when you threaten her child, it was just there for a second and it was gone.

"Sue show them where everything is then show them out." Sue was the one of the eyes of hate.

She showed us to a the wine cellar and then pulled back one of the cabinets and there was a hallway behind it with a another room and along the wall a metal door she opened and we where in Rambo Disney world. There was so much fire power in this room I could swear that Joe got a hard on. We loaded up and hid as much as we could in our pants, socks, shirts and walked into the hallway.

I felt a little chill, one that made my hair stand on end when I noticed that our little guide was no ware to be found. Ben pumped his shotgun and moved behind the woman covering our rear.

"OK so it's nice and easy on the way out everyone." Joe was way ahead of us.

All safety's came off and we slowly stepped back towards the entrance, the door of course was lock.

"Fucking little porno fuck." Ben should write poetry

It didn't look like there was any other way out and if there was it could take us some time to find it which we probably don't have because I doubted if they put us down here starve us to death. We started to hear something like a ticking, or the sound of walking but without a foot noise just a tick tick ticking, and lots of them. Then something pointy came around the corner and Ben shot it. After the shotgun blast there was a few seconds of silence, then roaring, barking howling, dogs and from the sound of it huge ones.

Not that it mattered, in this concrete cave the sound amplified and bounced around so much they could have been welsh corgis and they still would have sounded horrible. When the first one came around the corner I froze solid, the thing was about the size of bull, with three mastiff heads and totally black eye's, no white at all. It took Ben three shoots to get it down then four more came around the corner. We all shot at them, I'm sure I didn't hit any, my hands were shaken to much, but luckily more came after that and after that. We where firing and reloading for 5 mins when we all looked at each other and knew, if we stayed here we would just run out of ammo and die. Joe, had thought of it 4mins ago and had taken little steps forward every time he fired, he was way down the hall and we all had to watch not to hit him. Ben and I ran next to him.

"So which way?"

"Doesn't make a difference since we don't know what is on either side except more of the cute puppies."

"GO LEFT!" is was Pam, screaming over the gunfire and the dogs, we looked at each other and said what the fuck, we went left..

We moved like a turtle two facing one way two facing the other moving slowly firing and shuffling. My ammo was getting low which meant that everyone else was too, on top of that having to make it over the dead dogs and a floor with a of blood creak was slow going. I'm not getting eaten by dog, got remember to save at least one bullet for myself.

"Door coming up on right."

Joe was in the front and would hit the door first, the dogs where coming from all sides now, like they knew they could lose us. He shot the lock open and we all poured in with our backs to the door to hold the dogs out, but that wouldn't work for long. Julie lit some light sticks and we could see some bookcases on the walls that we rolled to the doors.

The I found a light switch I wish I hadn't, the bookcase are rolling cages, with like 50 little pit bull puppies in them all dead. Someone one here must have been experimenting with the bread, everyone with more then a couple of thousand dollars in his account thinks he is a fucking geneticist now. Pam started throwing up and so did Joe, me and Ben got really, really mad.

"Motherfuckers." I must be picking it up from Ben, if I live through this crap I'll have to back to school for basic communication skills.

"Well at least there is a window."

Joe had noticed a small window as soon as we had moved the cages he looking for a way out and not at the dead puppies. He started riping the wood off the window and Ben was helping, I was still to angry to do anything, Julie and Pam had squeezed their hands through the cages and where petting the little dead puppies heads. My hatred started to simmer down and I noticed some tanks with bio-hazard on them in the corner of the room someone had tied to make this room air tight. What ever they where doing to the little pups was happing here.

"Help me put put a couple of those tanks on this chair.." Again they looked at me like I'm crazy, maybe I am losing it, but the more war experience you have the more you learn it's a waste of time to argue with one of your team has an idea.

We all started running as soon as they hit the ground, I made across the street and pivoted started firing on the tanks. Whatever was in them was compressed and the blew open right as the little three headed doggies made it through the door. I hear them screaming but I better concentrate and catch up with the team, sucks when you can gloat..

"So were back in the same boat, low on ammo and running without a plan." Pam, as always, is just a little black rain cloud."

"Maybe not, the porno boy gave me an idea, I think I know someone that can help us out."

"Really, what is her name?" I wonder how Julie can keep up the banter no matter how crappy thing get.

But as always she was right, my first time, was with a girl from access the street, Harriet, she was 15 I was 16, it was over very fast for me and there was no blood on the sheets. Really the part I remember the most was her laughing, but I wasn't embarrassed. Somehow I felt she wasn't laughing at me or anyone, but at something, like the smile a kid makes when he finds out there is no Santa clause. I found out later that her step father and all her step brothers had been abusing her, until she ran away and spent some years living on the streets.

She wound up as one of the Magdalene disciples a group started out by a public school teacher on 9th street by a woman named Jenifer. She used to teach sex Ed then she moved on to the logical the only way to teach sex is to have it. The teachers union, which has millions of rules to protect their teachers but not one to protect the children, made sure she wasn't fired you let go of a teacher you get less dues, it was simple. They moved her from school to school even thou she always said she would do the same thing in whatever school she went to. Eventually she would up in ps91 in the on 110 street, where the legal system couldn't even get her out of the class room. She kept having sex with the boys and girls. Eventually turning the girls into prostitutes, before she found drugs and god, then they became whores with a purpose, which I think is worse.

For the first year the Magdalene's had a strict regiment, they couldn't talk, they worked on weighed hula hoops all day to make them as supple as snakes. At night the good teacher had a steady stream of clients for them, one after another. That's where I last saw her, in the school yard of ps91 on a horrible Aug day, it was about noon and maybe 100 degrees outside. She was as thin as a rail, her eyes dead and sunken in and with that pasted on smile that the Magdalene practiced so that they always looked accommodating.

She was working a hula hoop, a weighted 20 pound one, she mush had been at it for hours, she looked like she was on a meth and sugar diet. .

PS91 stopped any teaching after awhile, it became a new age whore house, tantra, the way of the serpent, all the quasi religions all fell under one roof, until the church of the ass wiped them, like everyone, else out. Shut most of them down except for the little school house where it all started, the girls here had took up arms to protect themselves, and the boys and girls from ass decided they would wait them out what's a couple of hundred years for them. So the ass cops the drug gangs, every one kept away from it. Magdalene also had there own little army of the escaped sex offenders, all paid in whatever way they wanted so they were totally dedicated. The perfect place to hide.

We are running as always, I didn't really know how hard it is to run with guns stuffed in every pocket and every crack.

"Let's find another apartment." Ben got winded pretty fast so he didn't like to run.

"No keep running follow me I have an idea.

It was 4 blocks away it was run down now, only the locals still came, most preferring the stylized church of the ass hookers. I remember losing my virginity in this building, just like most of the kids in this neighborhood. We got to the steps and the two guards waved us in, they were expecting us and that was not good at all, every one took their safety off. Up the steps which opened into what used to be the gymnasium and now is Magdalene office and court, and there she was sitting behind a huge desk made out of Mexican marble on captains chair and standing right next to here was our little porno friend.

We swung up our guns and the metal doors closed behind us at the same time some thirty guns pointed at us from the balcony.

One of the things I have learned in the last couple of days as I was constantly being threaten with one form of death or another is that when the mind believes, I mean really believes that there is no hope, strange things happen. The mind seems to go down an odd road, as if burrowing in on itself to escape. So now as some thirty or so guns that could rip through my body, all I can think of is the smell of the room. That weird amino and cleaning solution that is in every public school in the country, probably on the planet I bet if there are public schools in alpha centauri that same smell is there also. This building hadn't been a school in decades and probably hadn't seen a mop for that long either, but the smell was still there. I closed my eyes and waited for the pain, but the smell brought the memories of children running and playing and the hope of life on their faces.

"If we wanted you dead you would never have made it in the building." Years of training had made everything about her sexy, every word an invitation.

"It's been a long time ,Vic, a really long time."

## Remember as far as anyone knows we are a normal family

*Homer Simpson*

She didn't really walk, her steps where exaggerated, like a runway model, but whose purpose is not to show off the latest look from Milan but to make you want her. Julie was getting a little agitated, the woman here didn't wear clothes, well not in the sense we ware them to cover up. They wore them to, tease, to highlight a feature, to draw the eye here or there. My little friends breast were exposed and held up by a black bustier and as she stood there looking at me the nipples where very slowly becoming erect and she looked and them and then at me to let me know that she knew. The she looked over to Julie and then Pam.

"Ah still the same old Vic, making all the blood around you pump faster and faster."

"Harriet what do you want?"We were still alive and they had to be a reason for that, I hope.

"Still no foreplay, what a pity. We want to help you and we want you to help us to help you."

"And how can we help you to help us." that made here smile and she held the smile awhile for Julie who she noticed was the only one in the group who hadn't put her handgun away, it was just by her side.

"Let me show you something first."

She walked back to her desk picked up a remote and a video of our friend of the three dicks came up on the screen. The sound was pretty good but the video sucked, I looked like a gained 20 pounds squeezing out of that back window. Then we started to hear Helicopters, first your really couldn't hear them you heard the other sounds breaking up, but then you couldn't hear anything else.

When a helicopter assault team takes on a target the object is not to kill the people inside, sure that is going to happened, but not really the point. The point is to pound to location into dust, to remove it from the face of the earth. The 50caliber bullets came raining down on the little brownstone and some 200-300 miles per hour, some with exploding tips, some just hot metal but for a few minutes there before all most of the camera where destroyed it looked beautiful. Like a metal water fall speeding up time, so we can see the building that would have taken hundreds of years to return to dust, happen in 5 mins. Then the bullets stopped, the helicopters moved away and there was a profound silence, then some foot prints and a very pale man with incredible small shoulders dressed like he was going to a funeral, black slacks, red turtle neck, black shoes and one medal on his collar. The video stopped there.

"Maybe I didn't make myself clear." Her right eyebrow arched up like mister Spock, not a good thing for us,

She pressed the remote again and off we went to another grainy video but this time it was fast forward. It was what looked like a girl of maybe 15 or 16 and some guys and girls and all manner of gray shades in between were pulling a train, sometimes giving her water but never food. We watched as she withered and died like flowers is super fast motion video. Then as that last little breath was humped out of her they kept right on humping. The camera moved always from them to the chains that held her suspended in the air then down to the little two little tattoo's on her toes, little barb wire rings around her two pinky's toes, the mark of the Magdalene, covered in urine and blood. Pam looked away as soon as the video started but she couldn't block out the horrible sounds. Julie couldn't look away, held motionless until the screen went black, then she threw up and fell to her knees crying. But even while she was should could hear the little foots steps of that man with the red turtle neck and the little shoulders.

"Are we straight now?, good."

"Oh great one of your little whores gets killed and suddenly you want to take on the whole world. Sure why not, hey let's assume we are going to play along and that you can furnish us with enough guns to destroy a small swat team guarding this Davos. A team that I'm sure is faster, stronger and smarter than most of us. The question is how do we find this guy, the Davos, run every form of communication on the planet, no one knows where they are and where there are going to be. So I'm not sure if having your tits out effects your brains, but unless it gives you physic powers, we can't help you to help us."

Julie still hadn't put here gun away and you could tell she was looking for a fight, Harriet looked at her and Pam again and smiled.

"No I don't have that kind of power, very few people of governments do, but we can reach out to someone that does. Isn't that true Joe"

"Excuse me?"

"So Vic, you're transported under cover of darkness with other couples from all over the country to New York City. Where some of the most sophisticated killers on the planet are chasing you down with enough pull to keep the huge amount of destruction off any screen, server or mind implant. But somehow your little brother just shows up to help you, a little odd?"

Julie took the safety off her gun.

"Not only does he find out which city out of the thousands of cities in the world you are but once he gets here he somehow finds you in the miles of miles of city blocks. at the right time, mathematically, what are the probabilities of something like that?"

Joe took a step back and Julie pointed the gun to his head.

"Ahh Vic, so one to fuck and one with the brains." Harriet kept looking at Pam and Julie, she was really enjoying this.

Ben had been just kind of taking it all in until then, but I heard him putting something special in his shot gun, the pumping sound made all the guns around us go from semi-erection to right at us.. Me I was beginning to understand what Harriet was talking about and with the understanding came anger.

"Joe, what the fuck is going on." I knew, but I hoped I was wrong, I wanted to be wrong.

"Come on Vic, don't get crazy, just a little bet I got going that's all, no big conspiracy."

"Bet, really so what is the action on your brother?" Vic didn't answer he just stood there what that same 'I'm trying to BS someone face', I wanted to puke.

"Let me Vic, your brother might be a little shy in front of you. This little walk-about you and your friends are going on happens every year. It's run by the us government and monitored by the Davos group, I hear rumors that the Davos wants to shut it down, but who knows. Anyway, they keep the whole thing pretty secret, no news gets out, those who try end up with instant lead poisoning. Anyway, my grandmother use to say that the only way two men can keep a secret is if one of them is dead, so the word got out anyway. So every year big money, I mean GDP of small African nation type of money is bet on the game, every one betting on who is going to make it."

Now my hand has slowly moved to my 9mm, I couldn't fucking believe it.

"Well when you have that much money ridding on a game rules don't really apply, some guys try to get people on the board to tip the scales a little, right Joe."

"Fuck, Is that right Joe, you're not here to help me out, your just here to help a bet? How much you making on this, how much are you making to make sure your brother keeps getting shot at for some game. I hope it's fucking in the millions, that's what it's going to take for you hospital bills."

My mind was tunneling now, the anger blocking out reason and understanding, blood was all I wanted.

Harriett was looking at Julie who still had her gun pointed to Joe's head and smiling..

"So, sweetheart are you going to ask him or do you want me?"

Ask him what, what the hell else do we need to know? Julie looked at me with an expression I have never seen before.

"So Joe, who are you here to help?" What, of course he was here to help me, who else could he be, no, it can't be.

"Joe, answer her Joe." I was screaming now.

"Yes Joe answer your brother." The smile on Harriett's face was like looking at the face of hell.

"I'm sorry Vic, the odds were against you, because of Pam." He couldn't look at me, I pushed Pam out the way and started punching him over and over again, as he moved back, blood came out of his nose as he fell to the floor. I started kicking him until all I he was curled up in the fetal position most guys make when the hit the floor, protect the head protect the jewels. Ben finally pulled me off him and then Pam started kicking him, then he pulled her off.

Joe is bleeding and moaning in a little ball position when Julie walks over and puts a gun right to his temple. If this has never happened to you, it's as close to being on that line between the here and the hear after, while still being on this side. You can feel all your blood, your hart, you whole life pulsing at your temples against steel.

"Vic, if you have any control of your bitches, tell her to stand down. It's only because of him that you made it this far and without him your dead."

Everyone turned their heads to Harriet and I saw Pam take just the smallest step forward.

Harriet, as she is skilled at doing, said exactly the wrong thing, the one thing she knew would most likely make everyone start firing, the smile on her face was putrid.

"Well Joe, I got to hand it to you, your whole family is just as much a pain in the ass as you are." With that Julie stepped back and put the gun away, she knew what Harriet tried to do and wasn't going to fall for it.

It took awhile and he looked like shit but Joe got up fixed himself up and didn't say a word.

Harriet was watching us the whole time.

"There is someone I want you to meet, come with me."

We followed like nice little children, but I felt I had to close my self down just to hold back the burning desire to kill my own brother. There were still a lot of guns pointed at our backs as we walked down the very dirty and narrow steps down. The one thing I really never understood about criminal why they are so filthy. I mean if you can afford 10 grand for rims on your nice little Bentley, can't you have a woman come in once every two weeks and clear up the cigar buts and get the skank smell out of the rug.

We reach the basement and there are broken pipes spilling everywhere on the floor, rats and roaches and very close quarters which I don't like even when there aren't little red laser spots on my back. After 10 mins of walking and holding my nose we reach a huge rooms with piles of rotting something which go up almost to the ceiling. The rotting whatever is stacked in two walls like parenthesis, we start walking towards the opening and I have to ask.

"What the hell you have down here, rotting garbage?"

"It used condoms years' worth." Harriett didn't even stop walking, like it was normal to have mountains of used rubbers and sperm gathering in abasement.. Yeah sure everyone does it, there right next to the lawn mower.

"Oh ,no no, what the fuck, come on." For the first time Ben got it right.

The other side of the parenthesis has an old school furnace against the wall and sitting down in the center was a woman, another woman I knew. I don't speak Spanish often, mostly because I don't speak it well and my inflection is

American so when I speak Spanish I sounds a lot like Yoda to Spanish people. Yet there are some feeling that English simply cannot convey. So instinctively as I saw this woman in white pajamas sitting in a middle of an a drawing of an eye which is in a triangle, in a circle in blood on the floor. Three candles in front of her, I spit and say Bruja-witch Witch in Spanish is not the nice Wicca new age, woman who just wants to do drugs and get laid, ware funny robes and play with crystals. You'll find a Bruja, at the cemetery on Christmas night swallowing the ash of dug up bones of virgin children and blowing jackals. This one was my cousin.

## "I'm not a witch. I'm your wife"

*The princess bride*

"So, Vic and Joe, back in the old neighborhood and by the look on your face you still remember me, how touching."

"Last I heard you where hooked on heroin, I would have respected you more as a heroin addict." I never like the witches, seems like con artist to me.

"Still playing tough, remember that time my brother William beat you so bad you were crying like a little bitch. Ah those were the days my friend we though thought they'd never end, we'd sing and dance forever and a day."

My cousin Frances still had that annoying habit of breaking into lyrics.

"So, what have you sold these poor prostitutes on and why did you get me involved in it?" I knew now we were here because she brought up here, but I don't know how. Maybe Vic and her are working together. Fuck I wish I was an orphan and didn't have any family.

Pam, was somewhere else, her eyes look like she is hypnotized, she always was suggestive, probably one of Frances tricks.

"Have you ever heard the story of the town of St Luis?"

"No and I don't want to, listen you got these spread legs feeding you and giving you a place to live, that's great but don't try to sell me one of your stories."

Someone hit me on the base of my spine with a rifle but, I was down on my knees in a second and the rest of my group sat down around me.

"St Luis was a little town in southern California like hundreds of others., one the Neva raza had flatten on the way to LA.. Months after the rain of death that fell on California soldiers went sent to all these little towns and you know what they found. Death, dead husbands, dead wives dead children cats dogs fish plants even every blade of grass was dead."

Except for St Luis, in that one town they found every child alive and well, if a little hungry. Years later a student found the footage and saw all these children living and she got a little curious. So she punched up the satellite file, the history like all of the worlds history being stored safely in earth orbit with it's huge moon data storage backup, to see how it could be and what he saw made her cry.

The neva- raza was genetically superior, heavily armed and trained. These people, bus drivers, gas station attendants, accountants, stay at home moms. With some hand guns, old shot guns and a few rifles fought them. They knew they didn't have a chance, but there they were, throwing Molotov cocktails, ramming trucks into them, attaching them with dynamite strapped on their back. They all died but the nevea raza was on the way to bigger fish so they decided to go around and that saved the kids.

"Up to this point it's just tale courage in the face up overpowering odds, beautiful but nothing that we haven't all heard before. But this student went little further and followed up on the life of 11 of these survivor kids and found something interesting. Each one of these kids was special in some way, all scoring higher than normal on Something or other, some in math, some in motor skills, and some were even physic. Now There gifts did always pan out for them and some lost their lives to drugs and alcohol, but each did have a gift."

"Which brings us to why, why did these kids excel? There were a million theories each as far fetched as the next, but the one that panned out was the pure love principle. People married and have kids for a lot of reasons, but sometimes the two parents really love each other, not the, we will have a great life with money in the bank and a green back yard kind of love. No sometimes it's that I will jump off a cliff for you, , the waiting for 30 years for my love to come back to Ithaca kind of love. Now when both of these parents feel this, the child born from them a little.

"Is there going to be an intermission, because I have to pee and I'd like to get some rasionettes" Julie was already sitting down so she just got a light kick to the head.

So our student wondered what would happened if two of these kids born of love fell in love and had a kid and how far could you go with it? He used a simple hack program to hijack unused computer power from cars, TV, every little device until he had his own little supercomputer, which is what he need for the analysis. He found it took about 2000 years, about the time from Moses to Christ of couples who love, having children who love. After that time a critical mass of gifts is reached the child born then is really different that and will change everything. He called it the pure love principle

Pam eyes had rolled into her head, she had fallen into a trance of a convolution I couldn't tell which, but she was crying laughing, rocking and holding herself with her arms.

Julie was bleeding with that patented look of hate in her eyes and my brother and Ben where trying not to be noticed as they looked for a way out. I was getting this little itching in my brain, like an idea, that my mind really did not like and was trying to remove but couldn't.

"Sooooo, the government got a hold of this little student did they?" It was that icky idea finding a way out and making Julie smile.

"So they pick up newlyweds from all over and go after them to find out which ones are really in love, so they can someday get this kid?"

"Vic, woman always say you're just a good fuck, but I always knew better." Pam and Julie both twitched at that and every noticed that they did, my stomach felt like I just gad 30 hot dogs.

"The government it trying to get it's hands on that last little bit of human existence that had always been out of their reach, that has by its very nature been a destroyer of Governments. They want to produce their very own messiah, son of production, he who will finally destroy the dream of individuality, a king-of-king of consumers."

"Mother fuckers." Julie was playing along, doing whatever it took to get us the hell out of here.

"Yes, and father fuckers to, which finally brings us to your little group."

"What, It's over I thought this was some kind of magic to boar us to death." When Julie didn't like someone there was no way to keep her mouth shut even if like now she got another crack on the head.

"Imagine if it's true, the amount of variables that would have to be perfect to make it happen, generations, thousands of people all linked in a chain they don't know exits civilizations raising and falling. What if someone get into a car accident, or gets a cold or a headache and don't feel like putting out that night and it's all lost, or maybe one will have a bad taco and die or get hit by a falling piano. The probabilities are in the trillions impossible to calculate.." Ben's father was a mathematician, he hates him because he had no vices and as we all know only people with vices are truly loved, but sometimes against his own will you could see his father coming out of him.

"So they have been successful, that is way we are here?" Pam came back from wherever she was, well almost..

"No, the very nature of the improbable cannot be controlled, but they did get the time and place right, the baby is here now."

"Why here?" as I listened, really listened to what we were talking I felt maybe Pam was coming back maybe I was going some strange far away place.

"It always comes in the heart of the old world, destroy the heart and the body will die."

Pam and Frances ware standing in front of each other, there was something else going in that it felt, like being close to high tension wires. There were elements power, power that could turn you into a little ash pile

"Listen, someone better tell me what we are going to do, or I'm just going to blow my brains out just to get out of this fucking used condom heaven." Got to had it to here Julie held her tough as long as she could.

The 3 dick spoke now. "The child is in the Bronx, you must get the child and get him to into New Jersey, someone will be waiting for you there."

"Oh fuck this, listen we have only been in this city for two days and have had nothing but world class killers some human and some not trying to kill us. Now you want us to go into the Bronx, which on a beautiful Sunday afternoon is full of killers, but now I'm sure there will be even more coming after us and why? Because this want to be harry potter read that a collage kid made a statistical connection between some little town name St Luis and wait for it, the fucking coming of the messiah. Well just shoot me because I have heard enough of just shit, shit shit.

Our little three dick friend was going to take Julie up on here offer, when my cousin stopped him.

"Maybe a little food and something to eat."

At a formal dinner party, the person nearest death should always be seated closest to the bathroom.

*George Carlin*

We went to the roof which was still covered in iron, the old schools used the roofs as an outside gym before lawyers and video games destroyed fun outside. There was a nice long farm table with some candles and what anyone anywhere would have called a nice spread, it was a wonderful night and up here you could almost make out the outline of stars.

"There are still a couple of minutes before the meat is done, there are some showers downstairs and maybe we can get some clothes for you." Hookers had a practiced hostess vibe to them that made it, like everything else about them, fake.

Pam who had been somewhere else the whole time jumped at the chance and so did I. It was one of those nights I used to talk to Pam about, before she started drinking, how the day can start with your life hanging on a thread and you can end up dressed, a nice dinner with candles gently moving in a breeze. Surrounded by friends, family and strangers the stars smiling on you all from millions of miles away. The amount of things that have to be just right for a simple dinner to exist, makes one take the possibility of god quite seriously.

Joy is a shower, some new jeans and nice baggy shirt I am like new man. But even this new man couldn't help, to go over the all the info that I heard in the magic house of used condoms. After the Vatican was sued by the world court for crimes against the mind of humanity and folded it's tents like an traveling circus, you got used to cults. Everyone had a messiah, because you can't have a religion without one. Some cults had the messiah who had a nice house overlooking Hollywood and helping all the young girls find their way with drugs and cock. But the ones that really believed had one that was on his way, any day now, maybe next Tuesday.

That is bothering me, these guys didn't really have a messiah on location or one in the wings, they just wanted to make sure that the government didn't get its hands on one. I tried to come up with a reason they wouldn't want it I mean sure they would exploit him, maybe tax his miracles but would they treat him worse than the people who got their hands on the last one, doubted it. I looked over to Ben which brought me back to the here and now and to trying to find a way out of here.

"So Frances, where is this kid and how can you help up get to him and us out of NYC alive?"

"Do you know how many cults they are in NYC?" Great question with a question, going to be a long night.

"God no, listen lady can you answer a question without a story, I mean I know we can extend our lives pretty long but it's not forever." Julie couldn't just wouldn't let up.

"You know honey, the tough thing is hiding the fact that your in love with your best friend husband."

There it was, we had all been using that special form of self denial that only those raised in a civilized world can use. With labyrinths of language and pictures and memories and logic and, theology. But then the elephant roars in the middle of the room and we are all surprised, startled to discover that the elephant has reappeared with a aabbccaadraa.

Julia vaulted over the table, but to give Frances credit she knew it was coming, she was out of her chair and moved to the side. Julie fell to the floor were she was met with another bash on the head. The guy doing the bashing had a funny look on his face when he noticed the knife that Ben had buried in his rib, like walking into a room expecting a surprise party only to discover your girl friend blowing your brother, that kind of face. Ben got a crack on the head and was laid out next to Julie, Frances stopped her people from putting bullets in them both. They moved them to another room and for a couple of minutes I was left at the table with Pam all alone, neither one of us with anything to say.

Frances and three dicks came alone with our they're hardware entourage and quietly sat down, Frances put the candles back on the table and lighted them.

"There are over 7 thousand independent cults in new York city, from Christian offshoots to numerologist, neo-shakers and hundreds of superior races groups. They, we, have been at various stages of war with each other for years, no better than the drug gangs, we have never been able to get along, but we have found something to unite us. All the groups, from the fundamentalist tantrics to the shotgun disciples all agree that the government should not get it's hand on the child. We will all sacrifice ourselves to help."

Ben was impressed, the words that were never spoken anymore were we will sacrifice ourselves, no one did that anymore, for there god, or country or even family. He was not so impressed that he didn't see the huge hole that an over abundance of faith can cause.

"We will never make it all the way to the Bronx and then all the way back with a baby, if your one of those religions that believe in miracles then I can tell you it is a miracle that we made it this far." Ben, always problem solving.

Pam, as always asked the oddest questions. "Why us, there are a lot of other couples that I saw this morning, why not one of them."

"There is only one other couple besides yourself left alive, them." The old farm table was just a image, it changed briefly to a stainless steel table, which is what it really is, before an image was displayed. It was that black couple, I knew we were going to meet again.

"We don't know if their a legitimate couple, always one ringer put in with the couples they try to connect with the other couples before they kill them. We can't find any back ground on them past five years, they could just be very poor or there identities' could be created. As far as making it to the Bronx, you don't have to, the baby is here, so you just have to make it the twenty blocks or so tot eh bridge." So the guy with the three heads was in charge of linguistics, interesting.

"My experience with religious types, yourself included, is that they talk a lot but once there is pain involved they head to the hills."

"The sacrifices have already begun, look."

> No one laughs at God, when the
> doctor calls after routine tests.
>
> No one's laughing at God when it's gotten real
> late and their kids's not back from the party yet.
>
> *Regina Spektor*

It was like watching big foot and the jersey devil in a cage fight. Two creatures that up to this point you mind had filed under doesn't exist suddenly on tv. Johnny apple seed's is there full name but everybody calls them seeds. Ten years ago they got a hold of a genetically mutated seed that grew trees stronger then oak 20 foot high in one season. They completely destroyed Baltimore, trees where growing through concrete and steel and anything else that stood in their way. The CIA, NSA, homeland security, Dea and every other covert group with an acronyms chased them in every nook and cranny of the county. Not because, they killed a lot of people as Baltimore was slowly taken back by nature and not because of the billions of dollars of property values lost. It was because the seeds where the first group on the planet with genuine home grown private genetically altered weapon, a really good one.

The Ladies are trainees of the Davos group, they call them The Ladies because the recruits are all from 11-17 years old and they are required to where pink shirts. They are thrown into any battle that has overwhelming numbers against them, with, the one requirement is that they have to hide their tracks which leads to the white gloves they all were. But since no one had ever see a Lady people used it like a joke, if a kid in middle school suddenly vanished, someone would say he became a lady.

Here they where, two groups that didn't exist fighting in the middle of a New York street their fight to the death apparently making them oblivious to they mythological status. The seeds fought only with hand carved wood sticks, each one loving carving their own . Some as large and straight as a Japanese Bo staff, some just pieces of tree with the knots and all still on them. The ladies where like a 1950's street gang, one guy was avoiding the swing of the stick and stepping in and hooking the guys in the head with brass knuckles. Another had an ice pick and would sneak up behind the boys and stick them in the liver, but one of the seeds got him, his head cracked and his face was covered in blood. The seeds viscousness was odd to me I had heard they loved the earth so much, apparently there love did not extend to the humans.

Organizations, gangs, army's or multinational corporations bring people together for different reasons. Some want a feeling of belonging, some money some power, as many types of people they are in the world, that is how many reasons. But each organization has the believer, those individual that have dedicated there lives to the cause, they are the organization. There on the street you could see in them in the center of the riot, two believers facing each other. The eyes lock in an embrace deeper then lovers and with a blackness enough to eclipse a millions suns.

The Davos was a burley boy of maybe sixteen, his pink shirt and white gloves now covered in blood. He didn't have a weapon, he preferred to kill with his bard hands, and he was good at it.

The seed looked like a little girl and almost naked now, she had one long stick that she had engraved with a circle with a dot in the center, a cross and a star and she pointed it towards him. When believers meet; it's like lovers, not drunken sex, but lovers who are going to give their souls, who will expect no mercy, who believe that the one who wins is the right cause. They where, starting to circle each other slowly, the abruptly the pink shirts where called off by an unheard command.

But it was two late for these two, the woman tried a simple smash down ward, the boy sidesteps grasped the stick with his left hand and breaks is with a chop. Then he holds up his glove to show her the symbol of The Ladies, the half-moon with both points facing up, the snake and the skulls and cross bones. He followed up with a kick to the stomach but she caught his foot and spun it. He fell face fist on the concrete and rolled and got back to his feet. There eyes where locked again but this time he obeyed the silent command and with the rest of his team.

We stood there watching all the rest running away, no one even breathed.

"So you have about twenty blocks to get to another one of or safe houses, my people will help. After that you better hop Joe's contacts are good and ready"

I was still looking out onto the street and the last little filaments of the impossible, but the 3 headed mans words were bringing me back to reality. My plan was to let them believe that we where oh so totally on board with whatever they had going on in their little tiny little minds so we could get outside and get out of here.

"So rap the baby up and let's get going." Looks like Ben is right behind me.

"Baby?" Frances was not

"The kid, the chosen one, whatever." Even Julie had be silenced by the impossible battle below, but the mouth was back.

I was taken alone, to a room that was full of candles placed on the floor where millions and millions of circles, crosses, stars and symbols I didn't knew where drawn. I knew, like a baby knows who is his mother, I knew each one was written by hand. Each symbol infused with passion of it's maker, it's own personal magic. I always envied these people, they really believe there is something else besides money, sex, food and shit, something somewhere in someone, I hope they are right.

I kept walking, I was lead past 21 concentric circles of people sitting and praying and here too, you could feel something. A businesses man still in his blue suite, a biker shinning pierced lip nose and chains, reflecting the light as he moved back and forth, a hooker, a fireman, a taxi driver, a cook, even the occasional politician all here.

"Who are these people?"

"People who believe, they stay for an hour then they have to give up there spot to someone else who wants to join"

We walked pass rows and rows of flowers, there innocent simplicity shocking my eyes and my soul, I couldn't remember the last time I saw a flower. Yet here in a house of whores a few floors above a sea of used condoms there they were. As always, waiting for us to look at them and unburden ourselves of the endless ugliness we have created. Finally, there is a kid about 12 or 13 in the standard unalterable American uniform that no one is allowed to deviate from, blue jeans and a t-shirt. Which always makes me smile, for all their endless pre-teen angst and endless ,I'm different you don't understand they all dress exactly the same.

He was playing some video game on a hand held device; Frances told him it was time to go and he got up and followed us without a word. I walked behind him on the way out past the flowers and the rings of believers they dropped to their faces as he passed by. He never looked up.

"What his name?" I asked Frances because the kid looked like all kids playing videos, he was in his own little alternate reality and the most important part of that dimension is that it really, really, must not include grown ups.

"My name is Bob, not really a messiahs name I know , the guys tried to change it to all kinds of things, even started calling me "A" for alpha for a week. I told them my mother and father named me Bob and since I really didn't get anything else from the drug addicted bastards, I was going to keep it.

"He still didn't look up, but I finally got a look at the boy, his name is perfect because he most uninteresting teen I have seen in awhile, no special anything. You can photo shopped him into any background of any rock concert he will fit in so well he will be invisible.

I met up with the rest of my little tribe, sans Pam, and they are ready with new guns and lots of lots of ammo, it took about 15 minutes me to get all ready and I got a nice snub nose revolver in a shoulder holster, pretty much useless this days with Walmart shirts having some level of bullet resistance in them, but I liked the feeling. Thee gang made fun of me with the antique, but unless you have used a revolver you don't really get it. They revolver made America and sometimes you need to use the tried and true, you need something anything you can depended.

Frances led us back to the massive doors and the kid was right behind us, still on his toy.

"A revolver, can I have one." So the game thing is a distraction, a way of keeping people at a distance, the kid is apparently engaged. I didn't answer but one of Frances believers where running to get him on, like the pope had said he ran out of wafers..

"Here is the address you need to make it to, about ten blocks if you go straight, you should assume they know you will be coming and will be everywhere. We found a way to keep the air power off you and we have snipers and lots of surprises for them all along the way. If you go off the straight route we can help but it's going to be much harder"

"That's what I remember about most about you, when I was a kid your inspirational talks. Whenever I felt a little to happy I'd call you and read a couple of books from Russian Jews and sorrow would return, because you can't go out on a Saturday night in New York City without it.."

The kid still didn't look up but the crack made Julie hysterical, after her laughter subsided, she walked over to Frances amidst the sound of a lot of gun safety's coming off

"Witch whore, if Ever see you again I'm going to put a bullet in the stinky wrinkled crater sized pussy of yours and by that I mean your mouth. I don't care who's cousin you are."

Frances, didn't answer she just blew Julie a kiss and walked back into the building. Four of her men slid the metal bolts and open the huge front doors, I was just happy to get out of the asylum. But the outside air was like a kiss, even after hundreds of years of dumping garbage into the air, the Hudson was still cleaning it out, still giving us fresh air, even when we didn't deserve it.

Joe, my brother was held back, they had told him that he would be let go when we made it safe enough away, no on believed it, especially Joe.

"Well back to our Olympic sprints.?" Ben was as happy to get out of this place, then Pam finally joins us and it really bothers me that I wasn't really looking for her and would have left without here. The guilt made me take a few seconds to really look at her and notice she was wearing a blind fold.

"Pam, ummm, we need to get going, want to take your s&m mask off" Again, the fact that she could have been using an s&m mask with someone didn't bother me, which bothered me.

"Frances says the thing that is holding me back is my eyes."

Julie again started to laugh, "Man can you pick them Vic, what do you do ask if they are mentally unstable and if they answer yes you ask them to marry you?"

"Baby, I know you're into the whole physic thing, but you can't run in NYC with people shooting at us with a blind fold."

"It's this way or the other and I can't do the other way"

We all looked at each there and you could almost see question marks and exclamation points in the air.

"The other way?" I couldn't help myself, the boy on the toy or who know maybe the toy playing the boy answered.

"The other way is to have the disciple remove his own eyes which is both a test of faith, and a test of his ability to vendor pain.. The blinding of the outer eyes forces you to rely on the inner, which in turn becomes more powerful. Use a muscle more and it become stronger. The ladies are on the way, we will not be able to avoid them, however if we don't leave in 5 mins we will die before we reach the other safe spot." must be a hell of a video game.

Pam started walking down the steps and not slowly, she looked like she didn't care if she fell on her face and Julie was waiting for it ,the boy followed her also always with his eyes on the game. The rest of us started walking down also and I asked myself why I keep calling Bob the boy and what the fuck had happened to me in that whore house to make me so suddenly introspective.

The ladies. . .

We started running our little marathon with out the little cups and writing on our legs continues The kid didn't give us any shit, he just put the video game in his back pocket and started running. In fact since he was much younger then all of us he was setting the pace and it was one I was having to really focus to keep up. We got two blocks and they literally came out of no were, up close I could see their faces. The Devos groups have a long list of criteria for the pledges the most important is cruelty, but equality important is their beauty. There angle like faces here and there highlighted with makeup made the tools of death that each had in its hand that much harder that much colder.

Ben started right away with incendiary rounds, hitting as many of them as her could, sometime going for the cars in the street, they would burst into flames taking an arm a leg or head as it went. They just keep coming, chanting, the stories I heard from my childhood all come back to me, my heart racing. Like running away from the millions of demons assembled to hear the grate con man speak in paradise lost, they just kept coming. We were all firing now, no need to aim they were everywhere and even if they didn't have guns, it was only a matter of a tick or a tock.

I looked at the kid for a second and his six were done, so once in a while he would pick up something from the floor and throw it back. It looked like he was just chucking it but somehow whoever it hit went down and stayed down Ben got hit with something, just enough to slow him and us down and then they were on us, hand feet, clubs. I just kept right on shooting, even when someone grabbed my hair on the back of my head and slammed me to the concrete I kept firing, watch kneecaps explode, but never screaming never any sign of pain, just like the stories.

After a couple of stomps to my head, with my vision observed by my own blood and the endless shuffling of all those feet so hell bent on putting us into the ground. But then the shuffling stopped and there was an opening around me and they others, who I could see now, not to far from me. There in the clearing was that one I had seen earlier on the monitor, all cleaned up and by the looks of him happy as a boy on a Sunday picnic. The ladies was quite mad, a madness built and nurtured in there belife that there is nothing higher than want unless it's something he really, really wants. At this moment all he wants is to kill our little friend who is not even looking up at him, all this for Bob. The lady pulls out a dagger shinny and silver, not straight but undulating to a sharp point like a snake.

"With this blade not of this world I kill the future."

He threw it at Bob and Ben and I watched it, because it did move like a regular knife, if didn't spin but the point kept always pointed at its target while the rest of the blade moved like an eel, impossible.

Our friend never looked up, he sat down on the concrete right as the blade would have hit the center of his head throwing his toy into the path of the blade as he did. The toy exploded into a million pieces which formed a circle of tiny electronic parts and plastic around him and the blade came resting on his lap.

"Come and get it, or are you afraid to be without your master ?"

All the ladies looked at our little mad friend, who looked all of the sudden, frail and frighten, imagine believing all your life in nothing, then watching Peter calling one of his own at a Macdonald only two tables away from you. The lady came running, screaming his eyes lost in the realization that maybe, just maybe there was something, somewhere that could be pure, something not touched by sex or money.. Something he had to destroy, something that had to be destroyed if his life was to have a meaning.

The moment he crossed the circle, the rage was gone, left outside and you could see his face mussels trying to do something they hadn't in years smile. He was happy for a few seconds of his life even as the serpent blade that he himself had sharpened with hatred every night, is piercing he heart. In his eyes you could see love, a love he had always , mocked, urinated on, or buried is released. Then he dropped to his knees and the light started to dim.

Ben and I looked over at the hundred of white gloves and all the hands and fingers that a few seconds ago only wanted to rip us and stomp us over and over again. Then the hundreds of faces circling us all turned looked behind them and as they did, Bob stepped out of the circle and started walking and as he did the circle started moving making a path for him and us as it started to move outward. We made it out the crowd in about 15 minutes and I jumped up on top a car to see what was going on.

**Hatred is as blind as love.**

*Oscar Wilde*

So we running again this time Bob is holding Pam's hand who is still blindfolded , mumbling and crying. Then Bob stops on a dime but Ben keeps running a few steps until Bob pushed him with his left hand, not hard but when you're running that fast it doesn't take much to derail you. He got "fuck" out when the brick wall about 10 feet behind him exploded and we all hit the ground, bullets just started flying at us, one hit a piece of a brick wall on the street which flew into my head.

I'm laying in rubble, on a hard street in New York City with all of deaths little tiny metal helpers flying past me as eager to get their work done as Santa's elves. I look up and across the street, right there next to a solar assisted lamp post with the Eco friendly light bulb, I saw Satan.. As I thought his name I heard him reply in my head, please call me Sam, no one but my father and mother call me Satan anymore. Then he laughed and laughed and started dancing to what sounded to me was a garage band tune. The bullets still wising by him, not touching him but ripping up his gray brooks brother suite somehow. Then he stopped looked at me and spoke to me in my head again ,you know my father and his son, but you ever ask, where's my mom'? The bullets stopped and all I hear was, the ringing in my ear and that question, where my mom?

Then Ben yelled. "Dron snipers, looks like a fucking million of them on this block, we have to go around."

Bob Answered, "If we go around it will be more difficult."

"More difficult how, there going to sing crappy show tunes to us while the kill us.'"

"Like I said more difficult, we can make it through this way."

"Listen Bob, I don't know how many Drone snipers' they have in your little video game, but let me explain to you what they are. They are big boy snipers with a range of about a mile and a half, run by a computer brain twice as powerful as the shit that's running the entire Hubble telescope IV. One top of that it has a video system that can dance through the light spectrum or radio wave or x-ray, with audio that can pick up a cricket jerking off from 50 yards. All of this dedicated to the one sole purpose of shoving a really big piece of metal up you ass at close to the speed of sound. I've seen one, just one suppress a whole neighborhood of the take me to Allah boys. So unless you're going to add raise from the dead or burning pillar of fire to your repertoire, we are fucked."

"Computes think like computers, not like people."

Ben was going to start another one of his, I have to say amazing colorful rants, but Bob interrupted him with a simple

"Stop, time to go, please get up everyone."

Ben stopped and we all got up, even me with my bleeding and pounding head.

"Come on everyone time to dance."

I never liked dancing, I always thought it was almost something, almost fighting, almost sex, almost a sport.. So at the mention of the word dance I see club people, on drug holographic masks covering there faces, orgies and of course dancing. Yet as I rose on command, my body wasn't mine. It's an odd sensation to be in your body and see and hear and feel but have no control over it, you feel like a passenger in a taxicab made out of meat, meat that used to obey you and now doesn't.

We turned the corner and we all started dancing, insane, manic derisive, movements with no rhythm, no connection no logic, no reason. The bullets where flying past us, millions and millions of rounds. I was happy my body was no longer my own so I couldn't tense up of freeze still the fear was there. I suppose it like being thrown out of a plane, where the fear comes and still you keep on falling and falling and falling. I wish I was blind folded like Pam or mad like Bob, of maybe just dead anything to not feel this soul crushing fear.

Then vaguely my mind started to hear it, a rhythm not out in front there, but more like a a back beat or pattern. Well I could feel it changing me, taking control like the way your brain patters change when you listen to Beethoven. You mind understanding what you can't hear, but know it's there. We were the un-logic, we were moving a against it, against the pattern of the machines movements, breaking the drones aliment with their programmed view of what reality must always confirm to. Even their myriad advanced optics and there primitive but effective intelligence which was constantly readjusting to each moment. But without a reference, without some pattern they are always just a little behind us. Shooting between fingers, blasting off a lock of hair, firing through pants legs. Like a computer trying to analyze the joy of a child who just learned to ride a bike without his father's holding on. They can understand the physics of the bike and all the parameters of motion, but they can't even see let alone understand the joy.

Then suddenly the dance is over and our bodies once again become our own, I am filled with wonder as I can simply move my hand as my mind commands. Julie is not filled with joy, she slapped Bob across the face with one off those slaps that bring the hand way back first, almost knocked the kids face off. Then she started punching him, Ben and I just watched because we all thought the kid had it coming, Pam jumped in front of the kids and took a couple of shots before Julie stopped, the woman didn't even put her hands up or show any pain. I don't know if whatever the blindfold was suppose to do was working, I do know she is changing, or maybe changing is not that right work, more like unfolding.

We found another apartment and huddle in, this time we didn't have to threaten or tie up the occupants, Bob just told them to sit down and they did. We huddled in the kitchen as always trying to process what just happen and scrounging for food, then Ben asked the question I couldn't bring myself to ask.

"So magic?"

Bob found the kid in the house had one of his little video games and he was playing it again and not looking at the real world. When I pointed out to him that stealing was hardly becoming for a messiah, he told me it was and exchange but didn't say what he gave the kid.

"Nature has no physical laws, only very strong predispositions."

"Oh now, you're getting cryptic, is there a Yoda school where all the want to be messiahs go to?"

"Cryptic? Tell a kid that his baseball follows a certain path because all objects in space have a certain mass and a gravitational field associated with it and he will say your being cryptic. Maybe the child is just not ready for the answer, so yes it's magic."

The rest of our team started laughing, the kid had shut Ben up, I'd had seen Ben mouth off to a guy that had a snub nose revolver on his temple so this was no small feat and his face was hilarious. I could see in Bob's face that he didn't mean to insult Ben, he was really trying to explain himself in a way Ben could understand. He was also very used to the face that people wouldn't understand what he was saying, maybe they never have, maybe they never will.

"Guys, we need to get more ammo any ideas."

"There is a stash of ammo in the basement of this building, there is a stash of ammo and guns in every building along our path to the bridge."

He still didn't look up, but it was getting on my nerves that this kid obviously knew more about what was happening to us then I did. We all got up to go to the basement.

"Julie and Vic you two stay up here." Again the kid was giving orders, this time I didn't even answer I just kept walking until my legs stopped moving.

"You two need to stay up hear, I'll ask the Ruiz family to help us with the lifting.

It took me awhile to figure out the Ruiz family was the people sitting calmly in the bedroom, I was just about to go on a wild triad on the kid when Julie cut me off.

"Vic, let's just stay I don't want to go through that whole position thing again, please."

The strange group went down to the basement, strange supposed captives where happier then the captors. Julie and I walked into the living room, I plopped myself on the couch and Julie sat next to me.

"So why the long face, don't tell me messiah boy is getting to you?"

"Bob, no. I don't know how he does the things that he does but I don't get the feeling that he can forgive my sins or yank me out of hell."

"So what's up?"

"Death, I know, we are all grown up and every one knows that someday we going to die. But that's part of the fun, you know it's someday, now I know pretty much what week it's going to be."

"Are you saying that were not going to make it out of this alive, because that is news to me."

"Don't be an asshole, I mean really, you have to be as supposed as I am that we made it this far. The part that is really fucking with me is the regrets, I mean there is so much I would have done different.?"

"You mean like those bell bottom jeans you used to ware all the time?" she was never good with this type of shit, she cracked a joke when my mom was trying to tell me my grandmother had died, didn't go over big.

"Asshole, don't you have any regrets?"

She looked me in the eyes and said "Yes I do."

Then we our lips met and time really stood still, they say time is like so much of the human experience, subjective now I know why. There are some woman who you make love to and some woman you fuck, then there is that woman. The one that makes you rethink what the meaning of both words are. They say the hart wants what it wants but the body has its own ways it knows when it has meet it's one.

I was just laying there fascinated with the way her breasts moved to the rhythm of her breathing when I remembered time and where we where and who was in the house. We looked at each other and jumped up and dresses as fast as we could then Julie ran to the bathroom and I ran to the kitchen sink. Just as I turn the water on I hear the foot steps as they come up the steps, I make sure I keep looking at my hands. I have never been good at hiding emotions on my face so I keep looking at the water.

Pam walks in the living room and even from the kitchen I can see her nostrils flare, she always had a good nose and if there is anything to the myth that your other senses increase when you lose your eyes, then she could smell it. Smell that sweet smell of sweat and juice and breath that is only made by two people.

Ben on the other hand was oddly happy, but then again he always was when he got a nice bag of ammo and a bran spanking new shot gun, two in fact. The Ruiz family went back the kitchen and Bob followed them bringing food, he treated them better than us, and I wondered way as I kept washing my hands.

Julie came back out the kitchen and she was radiant, no one talked, not been Ben, which made me very nervous, but if here wanted to go to the mat for this right here and right now I was not only willing but able to put him, my friend for 25 years into the ground, if only it gave me the possibility to just be with her one more time. This is how Camelot died and the walls of troy destroyed and the Clinton dynasty destroyed.

I checked my guns I look at the clock and it four o'clock which meant that Julie and I had been at it for three hours which brings us the question of what the hell was going on in the basement for three hours. As I look away from the clock Bob stares in my face with that wired face of his that makes me uneasy and winks, which adds the ting of horror to his face and my inability to even imagine what he is thinking about

We hit the street running, no use trying to conceal ourselves now when every country on the planet has at least one operative with a gun aiming at our heads. So as we run it goes from strange to surreal when I look over at Pam who is keeping up stride for stride while the blindfold and without the Bob Jesus hand. Julie is smiling and Ben is frowning to the exact opposite proportion of her smile. I wonder if the you become the yin of a yang the second you say I DO or does it take years to be sitting on a couch with your wife crying at a movie that makes you laugh so much milk comes out of your nose.

We get about half a city block and we see about 50 subway rats, not real rats but that is what everyone calls them. When Roe V wade was over turned what was left of the progressive counted with states laws that gave people sanctuary if they dropped their child off at police stations firehouses churches. But it was latter expanded to so allow people to dump there kids just about anywhere. A whole generation dumped in and raised like wolfs in the subway's, there rules where really simple, do whatever for money.

I used to work the night shift in Fordham road in the Bronx and was crossing the bridge into Manhattan and looked by the water to see 20 of these subway rat with there tattered cloths and miss matched shoes corner a business man who must have been uptown for drugs of cheap pussy. The beat him into the ground until there was nothing that resembled a person, riped everything off him until he was a naked. Then most of the rats headed out in search of new urban prey but a few stayed to eat, really eat the guy. Right at that moment I made a mental note to save two bullets, one for me and one for Julie, which made me feel like shit because that extra bullet should be for Pam. We turned another block and there was one man in front of a microphone with hundreds of people behind him dressed in red. Davos red. pretty much by habit now we all cocked and ready but Bob put his hand out.

"So what happened to Jesus disciples when he died."

"They went out and preached the word." Pam never read a bible in her life, called herself a pagan and had a burning hatred for Catholics like every decedent of the English empire.

"Yep, that is the problem we had with Hitler, we destroyed his manifestations in this world, but we left the followers to spread across everywhere to poison the world. This one is mine, cover your ears, this will really hurt you if you're not ready and I can tell you, you are not ready."

Ben and I laughed but ripped off little pieces of material and shoved it in our ears, the one thing we have learned during this walk along the sticky banks of the river Styx's, just because something sound ridiculousness, doesn't mean it can't kill you. Bob walked down the block and I could see that they had set up microphone for him across the man with the man with the red shirt and black pants. He stepped right up to the Mic and started talking, his hand moving with his words, we couldn't hear him but from where I was it looked like some old school rap battle. They only difference was there wasn't a back beat or dancing and you could see the crowd's pain whenever Bob spoke. It looked like the words he spoke where getting inside of them, destroying the systems of the lies they had led.

Sometimes you could see Bob step back the words he was hearing smacking him the face and taking life from him. This went on for about an hour then the man in red and fell to his knees and so did most of his group, the rest ran holding their ears crying. The man in red fell on his face and didn't move, then Bob sat down next to him, when we made it to him he was stroking the guys hair.

"To spent all those years on endless logic and come so far away from the light, it's so sad. He had more discipline more passion then so many and it was just so fucked up."

He didn't say anything else he just kept stroking his hair and crying and we just stood there waiting not wanting to disturb him. We walked over the to group that had come, some where just sitting rocking back and forth, some had blood coming out of there ears, some had killed themselves. Every single last one, I swear even the dead ones, moved away from Bob as he moved, an instinctual move like when you move away from fire, you don't really think about it you body has millions of years of genetic memory, it doesn't need your mind for some things..

We must remember that Satan has his miracles also.

*John Calvin*

We walked and in the middle of an intersection we looked to the left and for the first time we could actually see the bridge.

"Give me a fucking break!" It finally came out of my mouth.

Bob was laughing hysterically.

The mind is set in its ways and expects certain things, like it you see a dog turning the corner you fully expect to see then end of a dog when it finishes its turn. But here was something that my mind was certainly not ready for. Men, dressed as bunnies, with cigars in there mouths and big strap on dilldos, other men dressed as ballerinas, with clown feet and shinny little razor blades, weaved into the long hair of the wigs. A regular, battalion of the insane, a woman, juggling infant babies, who where in turn each juggling grenades on and on and on. The mind and body froze unable to take in the endless impossibility, a man in a nice blue suit who's body stopped at his waist, the rest was a scooter, a woman crawling

141

towards us, backwards, her exposed ass sporting one pale gray eye on each cheek.

Bob, started firing, he had taken out the old revolver and was just slowly firing into the the land of make believe which apparently started right across the street. Then I felt something wet on my crouch.

"No fucking way." Ben had beat me to the punch this time

It was raining, rain from the street, up into the air, in little rain drops, falling up into the clouds, then there was thunder which to me felt like a underground subway where there is none. So this is what it's like to have a nervous breakdown, very dramatic, nothing like I thought it was going to be.

"Whatever was doing this was hiding in the crowd,." Bob was yelling, can other people be in your breakdown?

Could I single out which particular version of insanity was trying to kill up, I wonder if Alic had the same issues with the Cat?. I had been frozen there until a 5 year old girl in a pretty pink dress and paten leather shoes and what looked like a ugly tough piecing swung at me with an actual wreaking ball, I ducked and the thing went into the building across the street with the little girl behind it holding on to the chain. We where now apparently into the realm of comic books, maybe I would be killed by the rat with a blue suit and a upside down cross on its chest.

"The roach it's the roach." Had Bob lost it, the pressure of being second son of

I scanned and searched and found a roach about 6 foot tall with a Lincoln hat playing the violin. I started running towards it, him, whatever and noticed and Pam was right beside me with a machete in her hand, seems she wanted the very big roach dead. Then the roach started talking which made me start laughing enough that I couldn't move any more. Pam got to the roach before I did and went at it like sugar can, but it moved just out of her swings. It's movements elegant and smooth, like watching a giant roach in the new York ballet. Then it started to sing, an opera I think Una Donna mobile, with a voice so beautiful it unnerves me, but couldn't stop laughing. I just stood there immobilized by the absurdity it of all, the rules of what I had thought was reality suddenly no longer applicable, watching the rain fall on my crotch..

Maybe this was what madness felt like tasted like moved like, like a stone in the water questions started other questions, did I just prefer madness to the real world , was this just another form of cowardliness. All these question ran and ran and ran through my head as my feet stood riveted to the ground and my friends kept right on fighting, fighting for there reality.

Then I was hit, I don't know what hit me but it spun me around and I smacked the street with my face pointed towards the roach and his hoards. I saw Pam get hit in the face and went down hard and Julie went down right next to her. Ben was flung over me falling out of my sight and even in that weird semi-conscious state I smiled. A Puerto Rican killed by a giant roach, has to be a joke in there somewhere.

Oh of course, I got up and started running to a shoe store that was on the corner. It's funny when you're so zoned and you don't feel your body, you kind of just point it in a general direction. It takes me 5 minds to find what I was looking for all the while hearing sounds coming in from the street that were making my skin crawl.

I headed straight for the master roach, running as fast as I could with all kinds of projectiles being shot at me. At the last second I jumped up and kicked the roach in the stomach with my brand new pointy shoes. It froze the roach as my foot was stuck in its stomach, then it laughed and laughed and started to disappear drop by drop taken up to the sky with it's backward rain and it's legion from the madhouse. Until they where all were gone and the rain backward rain stopped, replaced by the normal rain that falls on tulips in the spring. I was looking up at the rain falling on my face and Bob, came into view.

"So, it's sad but looks like you're the brains of this operation." I heard Julie, Pam and Ben laughing and laughing.

"Even psychopaths have emotions, then again maybe not."

*Richard Ramirez*

Another apartment and another captive family, the world seems to be trying it's best to kill us in fun and inventive ways and all I can think of is I hope I'll have some time alone with Julie. At what point do I hate myself so much that I start running towards the bullets coming at me, it can't be long. I set on the bed with the nice Asian couple and their infant child smiling and trying not to point the gun directly at them.

Bob walks in and puts his hands on the wife holding the baby which makes them all freak out for a second, but whatever he is doing calms them down and they fall asleep.

"Come on we have to talk."

I follow him to the living room where the rest of the gang is cleaning guns and drinking and I look at them and can't recognize them anymore. These people used to spend most of their lives in cubical, starting at the scream and moving only their fingers. But looking at them now they look like the outlaws in old westerns, hard faces, hard drinking and no conversation at all. No one was mentioning what just happened outside.

"I called a couple of specialist for the next dance, they should be here soon so don't start shooting at the door as soon as you hear foot steps."Called, how could he have called, every cell phone in the city must be hacked in to listen to even a stray word about us.

"Who are they, food delivery I hope?"

"Molly Burns and William Reyes"

We stood there with our mouths open, it could have just as well have said Jack the Ripper and Lizzy Borden where coming for dinner. First you would be shocked that murders where coming to have some Italian food with you, then you would remember that they are both dead and they are still coming. We all slowly sat down and I took the drink from Pam's hand and swallowed all in one big gulp.

Molly Burns was a single mom from Alabama, one night this man breaks into her house and rapes her, she doesn't put up a fight because she figures once he's done he will go and leave her 12 year old daughter out of it. This was not the mans plan and after he finished with her, he spits on her and starts to walk up the steps, Molly goes to stop him. The rest if really the stuff of legend, with most of it I would guess being made up. What is confirmed is during the fight this man throws Molly out of here living room window. She hits the grass of front yard, grabs one of the glass shreds in her bare hand and jumps back into the house. The glass winds up in this mans neck while they kept right on fighting until he bleeds out. The police come a hour latter because one of the neighbors notice the broken window, and Molly is sitting on the man's chest with a knife from the kitchen, still stabbing him after and hour. No one ever figured out how many times she stabbed him.

Molly spent some time in an institution after that and fell off the grid as soon as she was released. Three years later Atlanta police got a box with a note signed from Molly which had the location of a man who was a known and convicted rapist, who was given seven years and was released on two. The man's balls and dick where in the box with the letter and the knife she cut them with. Seven years and three hundred men later Molly was still at work, some said it wasn't one person but a secret group of vigilantes, no one knew. She was revered as a guardian angel in some places with woman wearing little knives on their necks with a red M at the tip.

William Reyes was from about twenty blocks away from me in the Bronx. His dad, a construction worker, had married he mother Felicia, a drunk and wound up working two jobs to pay for her habit and all the medical bills that come with it. One day he got his leg cut off on the site and before he could be released from the hospital Felecia had filed for a divorce and took the kid. The court awarded her 80percent of the funds that he had coming in when he was working two jobs. The severed leg not helping him in the us courts that have pretty much mandated that if you're a man you a guilty and must pay. William dad, Pete, hung himself in the basement of his mother's house on Christmas night. Felicia was so mad that the steady stream of drug money had been cut off that she kept William in a little box in the living room. There he gets to see the endless streams of men sleeping with his mother and is abused by all. The school never reports that William never made it to school, the neighbors never report his screams and endless tears. One day one of their dogs get out and the neighborhood finds all these belt marks on the dog that get police to the house in 15 mins.

William is raised in foster care for a while joins the military and finishes collage, he resurfaces 10 years later. He called to police to let them know where to find a body of a Jennifer Gardner. They found her on the floor of Greenwich Village 8 million dollar loft apartment without a head. He had emptied out a pump shot gun on her face. It turned out Jennifer had been married 5 times and was collecting about 1 million a year in alimony and child support. She had sold the kids to Spanish American drug lords, but since the courts don't care if the fathers get to see their kids just that the checks are paid, no one knew. Two of the fathers where living with family one was living in a car, all had two jobs. Since then he has killed over 100 woman.

There was a knock on the door and they both walked in, Bob introduced them to us then to each other. It was amazing to see them together, swapping stories and techniques, it was love at first sight. I was repulsed at the eyes full of love, the holding of hands, like seeing Hitler and Mao giving each other's flowers on a spring meadow. I got past the little bit of vomit that kept raising up my throat, I started to wonder. When I was a kid my grandmother told me that everyone has to love something, that it was part of being human and if you think a man goes mad repressing his dark side, try to imagine what happens when someone represses there light

Here where two people that were on levels of utterly alone that few have ever faced, no government prison cell miles under the ground, no last man on the earth could come close to the feeling each of these souls must feel every day. Knowing that there was no one, no one on the whole planet they could connect to, no one now, no one in the past no one in the future. Each one going down that black highway of vengeance all alone, moving farther and farther from the light. Yet here they where born again in each other, like teenagers on a date, nervous, jittery, beautiful.

My group keeps far away from them, odd thing for me was how they looked, Molly was tiny, maybe 5, 4 and William had little round reading glasses. If I saw them in the park together I would think a nice couple maybe librarians at best, never the most notorious mass murders of all time.

"Enjoy the day, tonight at midnight you are the left hand of god."

Sometimes in life, you are have a situation where you are at a loss for words, watching those two walk into the bed room like star crossed loves, I felt my mind unable to think, or not willing, the contrast of love and murder to much for me to process so my inner eye was looking at the white screen of an empty movie screen, thank god. I sat at the window and watched the sky for the rest of the day, watched the clouds dance across the sky, peeping out between skyscrapers, watched the sun slowly, make it's move to shed it's light on the people on the other side of the planet. I was watching the full moon in the sky when I heard the door knob of the bed room I had tried to block out of existence turn and the two that made up the left hand of god, step out, their eyes alive with love and murder.

Midnight in NYC is more than just a time to party, might night is when New York becomes Gotham, with gargoyles and zombies and Satan walking the streets. The chain that held him in the pit broken long ago, now worn like charm bracket hooked to endless piercing. We walk to the police station and there covered by those who protect and serve are the guests of honor for the night. The ones who rape children, woman men, dogs in the back of suburban yards, sheep in the hills of Wales, all taken from their cells from lands of darkness called, Attica, Rikers and Evin. The cops had let out the worst and let them lose on the street.

At the point of the center of the cross walk the lovers of murders stop and pull out daggers, old Victorian one I can assume were picked just fro this day, there last day for them.. The two scream, horrible, hideous, monstrous sounds all heads turn to them, the police all walk back into the station turning their faces away from their sworn duty, from themselves.

"Stay single file behind me there will be blood and if you stray from the little straight road behind me you will fall into a hole that even I can't yank you out of." I don't know what the hell Bob was talking about, but I did what he said,

The two lovers two ran towards the hundreds and the hundreds ran to meet them. Soon, there was sparks of metal, gunpowder flash screams and rivers of rivers of blood. As we walked by half steps, behind Bob and tried not to see, tired not to hear to smell, to close the pores of our skin off from this Polaroid still of hell. Legs flew, teeth broke this made some of the prison men's puff up with full of erections. Molly would who was not covered from head to toe would jam a dagger in the erection first, then shoot them in the eye, always the left eye. We walked past the horror, I started to laugh a laugh at the uselessness of it all, at each splat of blood, intestine, brain, tendon that hit use made me laugh even more. Like a food fight in an insane asylum, the lunatics ripping there body parts off just to through the parts at each other.

We made it past the block of police cars with the blood raining down on us and I looked up and saw some officers in the windows vomiting. I saw the lovers slowly being surrounded, the circle growing smaller and smaller around them. On there faces was nothing but joy, soon they knew they would be free. The circle constricted to with an arms length and the lovers put the machetes down and looked into each other eyes for few seconds before it closed on them. Right when the last little bit of there life of the two was smashing into the street the windows opened up and the police opened up and the shades. Cars exploded, metal fell from the sky, the familiar sound of the man made thunder and flash of the lighting that gives death filled the canyon of the city street. The fierceness of the attack destroying the very street, chewing it up and mixing the asphalt with blood. No matter how many battles and bombs and explosives they send it doesn't destroy the memory of what they have done. The news will cover the prison break and the valiant police officers that saved our great city being overrun. We keep walking and no one in the city even notices that we are covered in blood so warm it's still steaming on us, no one notices.

Religion can purify science from idolatry and false absolutes.

*Pope John Paul II*

This time we hold up in a bodega, it looked like it had been out of businesses for quite some time. Luckily there was a sink and a bathroom in the back so we could clean up and there was still some can good around. Which was good for me because I hadn't had any Vienna sausages in quite some time and there is nothing that can calm me down more then processed meat and fat. I'm happy the place is empty and no one has to be held, I wish it was bigger so I could have some time to talk with Julie. We all sit in a nice little circle on milk crates looking at the floors and trying to forget what just happened and Bob starts.

"When I was 16, before I knew that I was the great and powerful BOB, I had a mother and a father. Of course later on I find out that I have a surrogate mother and a step father, but that's not really the point. My guardian's and I mean that in the literal meaning of the word apparently spent most of their life protecting me from a near endless stream of assholes that piece of shit Sam sent to kill me. I hear they even sent out of my nurse in the hospital to suffocate me in the little glass crib, sold her soul to be a super model. I mean really what kind of shit do you have to tell yourself to kill babies in a glass crib in front of whole families looking at them. But sure enough no matter how horrible the fucking shit is SAM will get some brainless shit to do it for some power, like fucking being able to race cars faster than anyone else or something else just as ridiculous."

"Anyway, it's funny how parents can keep things from their kids, I mean we all believe everything our parents say for years and years and even when we know what they say is a lie we still put a good spin on it. Who doesn't remember the year they found out that Santa Claus was just Mom and Dad drunk and creeping up to the attic on Christmas eve to put the presents under the tree and eat the milk and cookies."

"One day my father sit in the dining room and they say they have to have a talk with me, all kids know that whenever parents say they want to have a talk it's really you did something and they want to mind screw you for it. I wish sometimes they would have just taken a belt to me old school style it would be better than to listen to their piles of sanctimonious shit. But this conversation wasn't like all the rest, not like the awkward sex talk complete with my mom pointing to her crouch or the sad drug talk where they were really stern but twinkle in the eyes clearly pointed to fond memories of the trashed days gone past."

"At this talk they told me how they were some kind of agents who's whole job was basically to protect me oh and my whole life was a lie. They insisted that the feeling that the felt for me were real and my mother cried as she told me stories of being up all night pacing the living room floor when I wouldn't go to to sleep. My father reminded me how long it took me to finally ride a bike and the hours and hours he spent over that summer until I could ride, even I remembered my very first words as I rode away, I got it!"

"Bottom line my Dad and Mom were like super spays for the Vatican, which at first made me laugh and laugh. But hey were serious like HIV positive and showed me the guns and ammo to prove it."

"But my favorite part of the story was the end, apparently now that I was 16 I was a man and could take care of myself if I had to. They were going to leave me for two weeks to go after a couple in new York city. A couple that, and here are my moms the super agents words, were really not nice people. They hoped they would be back in a couple of weeks but there was a good chance that they might never come back. I don't think I ever cried so much as that day as my Dad packed Mom's really sensible luggage set into his Toyota corolla and pulled out of the driveway"

"So a week later I'm doing drugs on the couch with my girlfriend and some friends and we are watching channel 47 because Spanish TV when your fucked cracks you up. When a news flash comes on about a gun fight on wall street right by the bull statue that tourist come from all over the world to take a picture holding it's balls. So there they were in grainy night vision photography moving like Kung Fu Theater on Sunday morning. My dad was dancing with this other guy, my dad with a huge machete, which actually made a singing kind of sound as it cut the air.. The other guy had this really shinny knife that he moved so quick it looked like some kind of insect trying to find a way to get into a hole, but my dad kept moving and dancing and swinging. I remember my face turning red and hoping that my friends where so wacked they wouldn't be able recognize them, but they did."

"My mom was loping sticks of dynamite, dynamite! At someone that was shooting at her, my mom blowing up cars and parts of building and everything around her and this woman kept moving and keep shooting. Then one time the little stick of dynamite goes up in the air and that other woman shot's a car side mirror which smacks the dynamite back on the floor where it blows up in front of my mom. If doesn't kill her just knocks here some 30 feet back and slams here against a brick wall of a nice prewar building with pretty marble pillars in the front. She slumps down to the floor really slow, like he slumping was somehow synchronized with the footsteps of that other woman as she walks over looks at my mother's bloody face and started firing, slowly, like she was eating a cheese cake and wanted to taste every single bite. Until her clip is empty and she takes a few deep breaths. I thought she was going to light up a cigarette she was so turned on by the whole thing. They a quick jerky hand camera movement just in time to see a very large very shinny blade sprouts out of my dad's chest."

"The rest as they say is history, they cut my parents throats and rub the blood on the balls and horns of the bull live on every little web site in the world. I could feel my friends staring at me on that couch waiting for a reaction, anger, tears anything, but nothing came, nothing. The only emotion if you can call it that, I had that day was puzzlement, the word curious kept repeating over and over again in my head. I couldn't get over the faces as they smeared blood on themselves and this idol of Wall Street. They were just so young, maybe 19 or 20, they could have been sitting on this very couch or one of the millions of couch thought-out the world filled with teenagers on a Saturday night, but instead of staying in and ordering a pizza and a one litter coke to eat after they smoke a joint that decided to kill my parents."

"I spent years following their every move, the highly published murders, like the governor of Florida and ones that no one has heard of, like Lisa Ann. Lisa was five year old girl who was out with her parents at the San Diego zoo. They kidnapped her and tortured the little girl, I don't know why no one knows why, but I believe they just wanted to see how long the little girl could live. I came to finally believe the reason they made this whole public spectacle of my parents was for me to see it. So I could become obsessed with them and filled with a black and all consuming hatred for them and it worked. For 5 years I walked away from the great and powerful BOB, I was like one of those Goth kids but without mascara."

"I thought I got over it, but apparently not so much you know this messiah thing is not really a feel good job. I mean what would you say to Jesus if you saw him going down into a deep dark depression, hey dude snap out of it you have that whole die on a cross thing to look forward to. You see my problem, anyway I did put them out of my mind for a while until this week, when I found out they are here, looking for me. "

"I know all of you have a price, a mega lotto size, and price on your head, but I'm asking you, please. But if I have to die, and will all know I do, can I have one desire fulfilled, can you help me kill to the fuckers."

I got up first, but maybe by a millisecond, everyone got up, ammo check, shoes, knives, shotgun. Every other time we had made our way out of some little whole to fight whatever these shits though at us, the mind was kill or be killed, but not this time. This time the mind of the room was cool, steamy and dark, like a nice foggy London night and it had a name, murder.

It wasn't because we suddenly were believers in the great and powerful BOB, or that we felt like kicks ass killers all of the sudden, no it was because we knew; everyone knew who BOB was talking about, the idol worshipers. I don't know how they got their names but I knew how they killed. The man, Franco, killed with a shinny dagger that he made himself, the blade was made of melted down instruments that was used to performed abortions, the handles by the bones of the little infants he scraped up out of the trash of planned parenthood. The woman, Angela, killed with a simple hand gun, one of the guns that were used to kill those kids in Tienanmen square. She makes her own bullets also, made from the discard metals of the beds used in prisons.

They only killed those people that had the most promise, a ten year old piano prodigy, a kid from Harlem, that got a full scholarship, a couple from Florida that had actually waited until they got married to have sex. All the killings were very public, they would let the local police and media know they were coming to town but never who they were after. That is why we all got up, it was like someone telling you I can send you back in time to kill the guys who flew those planes into the world trade center, want to go?

"We can't all go, only two against two."

"Wait, let me guess, we going to draw straws, or better yet arm wrestle for the privilege of going off and maybe getting killed. Bob, do me a favor and next time you talk to your father ask him to make at lease one thing easy to do." Ben really didn't like Bob, I wondered how many people couldn't stand that little kid with the long hair name Jesus in home room.

"But he has, Ben, he's made it really easier for you to talk shit"

"Shut up, Ben, so, who it's going to be?"

Bob went to the kitchen and got out a box of salt and came back into the living room popped open the top and through the salt into the air. The salt went all over the room but when it all cloud cleared there was only Julie and I had salt on our heads.

"Julie, one day were going to have a little discussion on exactly whose is victors wife."

Pam was not happy, but come to think of it I can't remember when I last saw here smile.

"There is another problem."

"Of course there is, wait, we can only kill them with the fangs of werewolf born in Bedstuy "

"Something like that do you remember the Rey's phoneme?"

Paul Rey's some kind of logical guess since the age of five, able to figure out any problem. He helped toppled a county for the CIA, by pointing out the one person in their government that was really holding it all together, the minster of agriculture if you can believe it. Then at 20 he took a bunch of barges out to the Atlantic Ocean and lit up 50,000 barb q's which somehow, and no one but Paul knows to this day how, stopped the hurricane season in North American.

At thirty five he was at a restaurant in Paris when a Muslim man shot one of his wifes in the head because he had tripped over some shoes that their kids had left in the living room and fell on his ass. Unfortunately, she let out the faintest laugh, and as always there was something in the Koran that forbids it and the penalty was, you guess it death. Paul was about two feet away from all this and the blood of this poor woman slowly crawled over to his shoe. He didn't move his foot, he just started at the blood. As the police came and went and the restaurant workers calmed everyone down, hours later when other dinners came it. He was still looking at that spot where the blood had been. After leaving the restaurant he headed to the top of Eiffel tower and just looked out at the city of lights. He flew back to NYC that day and had a press conference, he announced that he was going to solve the last of the great problems, the mystery of god, or why there is suffering in the world.

That night at midnight the idol worshipers called into a radio station and announced that if Paul ever tried to announce the mystery of god, they would kill him. When they asked Paul what he thought about that, he says of course, I was going to put them out of business.

Paul said this will be a test for all mankind, if they really wanted to move forward, they had one job and one job only, keep me alive until I make the announcement. So the world went into action, security teams from every part of the globe, kept an eye on his food, the routes he walked, were he slept and who with. It took Paul 7 years before he came to the press again, in that time many died protecting Paul.

There he stood in the middle of grand central station, his hair white from wresting with the unknowable. Black shoes, black slacks and a black turtle neck on three king's day, and billions of breaths held suspended as he came to the podium. Each hart hoping against hope that finally, someone would explain the why. No one breathed as the shiny blade came out from his chest, no one moved as he fell to the floor and bullets rain down on him.

The day's months and years ahead saw an entire planet in shock, numb, until, as some expected, the anger came. As people looked to someone, something some group to blame. The world pored over every millisecond of the footage of that night looking for conspirators. What they found was really more shocking in its infinite blandness then anyone could expect.

The couple just walked through all the security, not with stealth or an orderly plan but by the tiny little mistakes and everyday distractions that everyone makes. Past the front door when the guards look at the ass of a passing woman. The next checkpoint as the woman was arguing with her boyfriend on her cell phone, even passing the central intelligence boys as they were focused, as always on a possible, Midwestern guy in the rotunda. Not one person stopped, questioned or even looked at them. The world of physiology told us that the shadow side of the whole world didn't want to die and so as the last revenge of the id, it destroyed it's destroyer without even uttering a word. The couple became a legend after that like vampire's.

"The worshipers are protected by Sam."

"Great, I love this more every second." Julie was getting her war head on.

"You can only kill them if they are in a circle, Sam can't protect them in a circle."

"So you're not saying we will kill them in a circle you're just saying we have a better chance if they are in circle and no change if they are."

"Yes, would you like me to make little diagrams for you?" Bob was losing his patience which somehow was really making my break out in a big grin.

"So they are in a building that is only 3 block from the Petra's circle, get them to follow you into the circle and you will have a chance."

"So, wife two, you ready or are you going to keep talking?" Ben gave me a looked but even he smiled at the wife two cracks.

Outside it had started to rain and if you haven't ever been in a rain in New York City you have no idea of how oppressive that is. When it rains in New York the world is stripped of all color and contrast. Not like a black and white movie, where they are crisp shades and lines, no all is gray. Gray is the water pouring down from the gray clouds onto the gray building and running along the gray streets. Gray is the lives of the people that walk slowly avoiding the gray cars that never stop. Gray now is my hart as we try to find some of the worst murders this world has ever created and yet I can't find that rush of red hate I so desperately want to have. I feel the gray rain seeping into my soul, drinking the intention and passions of my life, but we keep looking for them.

Prayer can be done in a lot of ways,with the voice, with the body and with a little shire. Sometimes people pray and they don't even know they are doing it. Dwayne is a kid of 11 who hated the fact that there was another child in the family. Every day he clutched on to his idol worshipers dolls, which he bought at k-mart in the mass murders section, right next to the marvel figures. Every day he wished they would come and get rid of that other child, his prayers were answered.

They came into their 2 bed room apartment at 3am, Angela likes to break the door down when everyone is sound asleep for the shock value it has, especially on the children. They will never forget it, it they live. Dragged from their beds in their pajamas with little unicorns and carton characters into the living room where they tied him up so all could watch.

There Franco fulfilled Dwayne's prayer and tossed his little infant brother out of the window, you could hear the baby cry, then a thud.. Angela held his mother down on the couch the man sucked all the mother's milk out of her tits and they both laughed and laugh and occasionally smacked her in the face. The boy cried and shook and tried to look away but the woman would kick him in the groin screaming.

"Isn't this what you prayed for, well here we are how many people in this world can say their prayers have been answered?"

All the boy could do was look out the window once in a while to sneak a look at the sky as his mother died of starvation and abuse in front of him. Then one time he looked out and saw someone on the fire escape someone was looking in a woman. She made a couple of gestures with her hands which the boy didn't understand then the she pulled out a gun and the boy rolled himself off the couch onto the floor. The bullets started flying into the room from the window non stop, moving from one side of the floor to the other like a sprinkler, trying to make sure every inch of the room was covered. Then it stopped, after the noise stopped you could hear things still falling of breaking or shattering from the hail, but it was very quiet.

Then there was the sound of running on glass and the idol worshipers, with out so much as a scratch on them, headed towards the fire escape, firing as they ran. They pop there heads out the window but return fire forces them back in. It soon stops and they jump out to the fire escape and catch Julie and Victor jumping to the street. They fire down, killing a woman with her groceries and making most of the people run. They say luck is zero sum thing, good luck for someone means there is bad luck for someone else. In this case the bad luck was for for the idol worshipers they also fired on a drug deal, so an entire car load of guys starting firing back at them. Which put the couple back into the apartment

"Who would think luck would be on our side for once."

Julie joined me and the dealers firing into the apartment but no matter how many bullets we poured into that window, a few shots came back. And that's what bothered me; it wasn't like two people shooting it were like one. The obvious answer came when shots started coming from behind us. Angela had gone around and was behind us, shooting and moving so we could get her location. She had that weird movement to her, like she was a semi liquid as she moved, fluid, unpredictable. Then the man came on the fire escape with the kid in his arms and just threw him over. The drug dealers froze, even for them this was a level of cold blooded they hadn't seen before. Julie dropped her guns and ran toward the falling child I was left trying to cover her from two different directions and it wasn't working really great.

"What the fuck now?" Some really intense fire started coming at us from to our left, bad enough to make the dealers leave in a hurry, those that could still walk. Julie came back after the poor kid hit the sidewalk and his head, there wasn't anything to save. She was trying to get a look at what was coming at us while not getting holes in that pretty body of hers

"Well, you're not going to like this Vic."

"I don't like it already, so give it to me."

"Red shirts."

We looked at each other and realized the only reason these "world peace" keepers hadn't reached us so far was because of Bob, he must have been shielding us somehow. He also must have known this little side trip would bring them out, I've never beaten up a messiah before, but if I live I'm going to. At least we were in a pretty decent cover, a little bit of concrete and some cars were keeping us from the main waves of bullets, but it wouldn't last long.

"What the fuc" There was more shit coming from behind us now, not like the hurricane in front of us, not pointed at us but accurate. Sometime amateurs will shoot at you with everything from a 9mm to rocket launchers and you deal with it because you know the mothers are just as scared as you are and are trying anything to kill you. Then sometimes you come up against someone with a little six shooter that really knows what he is doing, nice grouping on the shots, specific ammo and a great firing position, that is the guy that makes your bowels lose.

It was this second kind of fire that was coming from behind us, taking out the red shirts; you couldn't see them, not even the flashes of the guns, just the sound. Even the sound seems to come a second or two after one of the red shirts head exploded. Like going to the show in baseball, the pros are on a completely different level.

Whoever was putting it to them was creating a hole for us right over to the left, it wasn't a completely safe hole, but it was one, well that is what I thought. Coming at us via that nice little opening I had hoped to get the hell out of was the Idol worshipers. I guess when Sam has your back you really can take risks. I taped Julie and believe it or not she started smiling and firing right at them, it took me a while but then I got it. The two of them really couldn't move out of the little tunnel that much or they would get hit, so we had them. I started firing right in the center, sooner or later one of their body parts would have to cross the center. Now SAM has a lot of powers but none of them involve the actual changing of the laws of physics or so I believed. But I saw it with my own eyes, as they ran towards us they zigged and zagged, I've seen a lot of guys do it before. sometimes it worked for a seconds until you get what they are doing, sometimes it doesn't work at all its pretty much all luck.

Which is just what the worshipers had, the bullets would always just miss them and those malevolent smiles on their faces would just grow. Meanwhile the feeling in my stomach that we were not going to make it out of this alive just kept growing in my stomach. Everyone has a different reaction at different times to that feeling, me I just wanted to have one more egg roll, that's all a nice hot egg roll and some duck sauce and I would be ready to die. My mind starting thinking about the all the egg rolls I had ever had in my life as my own personal demons came closer and closer, the bullets always just missing, Julie grabbed my arm and pulled me up.

I was dazed at first, but I started running right behind her, firing back every once in awhile and wondering why they hadn't put some bullets in us long ago. But as I was running and shooting I looked at the woman's face and I knew I knew because I've had that face and everyone one on the planet has had that face at least once in their life. Lust, raw lust, they wanted to kill us nice and slow and enjoy every little drop of blood they rip out of us. They were not going to let a stray bullet to the head come in between their passion and joy.

I saw a line of the snipers on top of a building; it was the local swat teams, with their faces covered up but their colors flying. It wasn't just the NYC swat team, there was Philly, LA, Newark, Chicago all in on the party, all wanting a piece, but no one was shooting now, looks like everyone wants them to gut us also.

Then were crossing traffic and the cars in NYC don't stop or slow down when you cross the street especially this high up in Manhattan. Run down a pedestrian and there won't be any witness, because no one up here wants anyone looking into their past. America went the way of the Romans with a law against everything, so if you dig deep enough everyone has broken a law. When Jesus was asked "what have you done" the roman knew what he was asking, he was giving him a way out, for surely with all the laws on the books you have broken a law.

We made it to the other side and Julie stops and puts here guns down on a concrete bench, an invention of government bureaucrats, no song, no sonnet, and no works of passion where ever spoken on a concrete bench.. I couldn't help but stare at her, maybe she had decided to give up, I was going to turn around and let go of my last rounds when I see the statue. General Petraus, conquer of the Middle East, we are in the Pertras traffic circle. I put my gun down on the same ugly urine and dung smelling bench and pulled out the nice little ice pick that Bob had handed to me and turned around. There is a certain mindset that has experienced to be understood, murder. Not the kill to survive instincts no the other one, the desire to kill so strong it blocks out all thoughts, memories, light, red deep red, is all you can think.

The couple focuses on the ice pick and freeze for a second, then those smiles again.

"So how lucky we are today to kill the some more of the pussys disciples of BOB. I help he gave you more than the ice pick, maybe magic runes or crystal enema. Because I can tell you if that is all you have, you're going to wind up with that little point shoved right up the tip of your dick."

Julie was gone, further into pure murder than I was, she was just staring at the woman, the mental daggers in this case matched by the physical. Julie had raided her are about shoulder height so it was pointing straight at the woman's eye. I always thought those old westerns were stupid, people waiting for minutes before they started shooting yet here we were. I didn't know what I was waiting for; all I could fell was a red hurricane in my soul just going from category 1 to category 5, to some impossible number of hatred. There was a drop of rain, just a drop but it acted like a gun at the start of a race. Julie moved first, but I could keep track of here because, the man was coming at me fast. My farther Rubin, was one of those Puerto Ricans that insisted on he was descendent from conquistadors, which meant for me and my brothers Guitar classes and fencing. I spent 15 years, in fencing, you spend 15 years doing anything your mind might block it out, but your body will never forget it. So as the man jumps up to put that scalpel in my head, I do the standard lunge I have done millions and millions of times, my right leg out, my left leg straight, the force of my lunge and he forward motion taking the ice pick right though his hart. The little handle of the pick pressed right against his chest, the warm blood coming over onto my hand.

Shame is never one of those things that came easy to me, but that is what I feel as the joy of having killed this monster swells my chest. I watch his face and on top of the pain and the garbling with the concept of death there is something else on his face, a puzzled look. He is looking around for something and then he sees the statute.

"The circle, when in a circle, run we in a circle run."

Julie and the woman were on the floor grappling while trying to shove a knife in a liver or back. But when she hears he lover she managers to get up and start running, I move to stop her but the man holds my arm every as I start punching him with my other hand and more and more blood pours out of him, hold it even as he drops to his knees. The woman makes it right to the edge of the side walk and stops, looking at someone across the street. I could make the guy out which was weird it's not like he was that far or anything but it was like when you hold up a middle finger on TV and the ass the blur, no matter how hard I tried to focus I just couldn't. But I heard him, in my head and it made me start shaking, another person's voice in your mind can only be called the last violation.

"Kill them both or die."

She turned to turned around like she was going to run in the other direction right thought us bur she stopped again so Julie and I turn around and there was BOB. I was really hoping that I would hear him in my head because I don't like his voice even in my ears. Julie didn't wait she went right at the woman, slashing wildly, which was easy enough for her to move out of the way. I was scared now, I knew from countless fences matched when to know when someone is just waiting for an opening. I kicked the man down on the floor and yanked the pick out of him and raced for Julie.

The blade came straight from her waist with a downward thrust, going for kidneys, I went down on it, which forced her hand down, but would have left me in a really bad spot, and so I kept the going with the momentum of my arm and rolled out. Julie moved back and so did the woman; I was back up point my pick at her head. She was right in the middle of us and really had only one shot, so I got ready for it. She made her move for Julie, keep lunging and stabbing, Julie didn't know anything about knife fighting so she kept stepping back which would only help her for so long. But to her credit Julie started moving sideways which was taking just enough of the woman game to get behind her. She step back so her back was touching my chest which stopped my lung in it's before it was born, then she stabbed my right leg and jumped at Julie again. I made a flaying lung for her, not a sport lunge a fight with blades on the street lunge and got her right in the back. Julie took the opportunity to start stabbing her in the face. I heard gunshots and I jumped at Julie so we hit the floor with the dead body on top of us. It was BOB firing at the blurry man, one after another. The blur didn't move, but it did speak in my head again, "Kill all my children, you won't win." and he walked away, this time there was something in the voice that made me puke. Now the storm of bullets that we had run away from was catching up to us, you could smell the smoke once in a while when the wind changed direction and the echoes of off the building were getting loader.

**When turkeys mate they think of swans.**

*Johnny Carson.*

I finally noticed the rain, the senses start coming back slowly after your mind is in the red murder zone. I got up and picked Julie up and we started to walk to BOB, everyone else was their and I guess I hadn't noticed that I was holding Julies hand until I saw PAM and Bens faces starting at our hands. I started to let go, but Julie held on to me, I was glad she did. Hands can talk some time, I could see the Ben's hand closing and I knew what was going to happen.

Then his handed stopped and I heard a shot, I kept looking at his hand as it went limp. He fell to his knees and I saw the blood trickling down his face. I got one foot forward to move to him when Julie tackled me to the ground, when I hit I could see Pam's eyes locked with Julie. A war had begun right there in those looks, a war that would not end until one was dead.

Bob didn't hit the floor and we were all screaming at him, he was looking up, looking for the shooter. I guess the shooter admired him and came out and aimed right at him, it was my black friend from the start of all this shit, and right next to him his woman. I wonder is that what love is after all the ability to kill the whole world, burn it up into a nice neat nuclear blast so that the one you love can live and you can with them. BOB pointed a finger back at them, the building the shooter was standing on was a prewar, and by that I mean WWIII or the sand war. A tenement that had seen better days and owners that had taken better care of it. I want to believe that really it was only a matter of time before that roof was going to collapses, that is was unbelievable good fortune, that it happened now. I don't want to believe that BOB can wave his hand and make skyscrapers fall back to the dust they came from. We all rushed to Ben after wards, he had time for a few breaths, time to grab my hand and say.

"Asshole, you better take care of her, because I'll be waiting for you, you hear me, I'll be waiting for you."

I picked up Bens shot gun and walked over to the rubble of building and found the couple. The woman was dead; I couldn't tell if it was the fall from five stories on her head or the weight of bricks on crashing down on her and exploding here hart. The man was still alive his legs were broken and two of his ribs were sticking out of his body, but he was breathing, panting really. I started firing the shot gun shells into him, Ben had it loaded with incendiary, he always like the explosions, said it felt like he was shooting fire and brimstone. I fired again and again and the fire grew and grew and I could smell that burring hair and flesh I knew what he meant and I kept firing, even after the gun was empty.

"RUN." Pam, Pam, Pam, all this time, my love for you was just an over blown Florence

Nightingale syndrome and all it took was finding my real love, the death of her husband and the possible death of a messiah to make me see, Ben was right, I am an asshole.

We were surrounded, by the mother fucking red shirts; I'm going to kill as many of these country stealing fucks as I can before I go. But they weren't shooting, I heard footsteps clear crisp footsteps, which have to be impossible in this city, yet there they are. Maybe the sound was in my head, but it had a weird feeling to it, like something was on its way. It was a little man in a plain red shirt and black pants with shoes so shiny they seem to be generating their own luminance. BOB, started to walk out to meet him, like meeting a cousin you hadn't seen in years.

"Sam always sends dogs to do clean up, I tell you if that tailed boss of yours had balls they would be yellow. "

The little man clearly didn't like the banter, he just make a frown and pulled what looked like the standard big kitchen knife.

"You see, not only is the dog stupid but he also has no sense of style."Bob, held out his hand to me and I gave him back his ice pick, he bent down and started rubbing the side of the tips on the sidewalk, like he was sharpening it, sparks flying

"Whenever your ready dog boy." He looked up from the squat. The dog boy, ran at BOB with the kitchen blade behind his back, he jumped up right before reaching BOB bringing the blade up and coming down with all his body weight and holding the blade with both hands.

Bob sprung up from the squat and blocked the blade and the eyes of the dog boy went wide, like no one had ever blocked him before. I could feel the impact on the ground like a subway train passing by underneath. The dog man kept forcing the blade down so BOB starting stepping in on him until he had to back off.

"As always with SAM, he gives you just enough power to serve"

Bob started to attach first with a standard lung, which I thought was a little slow and not to discipline. But it was a trick, to get the dog man to come in and he did, then he stabbed him in both eyes and disengaged with a jump, I had seen the jump before but not the landing. There was something missing in the landing, I just couldn't figure it out. The dog man was screaming and swinging with his kitchen knife, powerful swings that could cut a man in half if they connected. Bob stayed a little outside of his range, then moved in and put the ice pick in his right ear. There was a lot more screaming then and Bob start taunting him.

"What are screaming about, afraid that when your senses are all gone you will have to look inside and deal with the shit pile of your own soul?"

Soul, a word I hadn't heard in a while it was so out of style with it connotations of another world that a government couldn't control or tax or take away from you. Bob pieced the other ear and the dog man started to run, but his own men pushed him back into the battle, screaming wailing, begging for that god of stuff to help. But when was the last time a Sam helped anyone, you would think his followers would have figured this out by now.

Bob was just looking at him and the crowd, then he looked at us, took me a while but I finally got what he was trying to "say". Once he killed the Dog man the red shirts will be on us like locust, each knowing that the one that kills us will sit right under the asshole of SAM himself, like a Politian or a mortgage broker. .

Pam and I started backing up, but Julie wouldn't move from Ben, she stood there looking at his body with little irregular tears flowing down her cheeks, like she was holding them back, Each tear making it's way past an almost super human effort to stop them.

Bob slid in as close as he could to the flaying bleeding thing and then worked his way behind him. The pick went right in the back of the scull, merciful I suppose. As soon as the body hit the floor BOB ran towards us and we ran behind him. I could hear all those red shirts breathing the dog man had made a blood thirsty pack.

So we ran again, this time it looked like it might really be the last little sprint. Bob didn't look like he had a plan, just running. Bob kicked open a door to an apartment building and we followed It looked like a good spot. The lobby narrowed in the back into a long hallway so they would all have to funnel into that, even when we ran out of bullets we could hold them off even hand to hand for awhile.

But BOB didn't turn around; he opened the metal door for the basement and ran down the metal steps. When he hit the basement floor, he turned to us.

"Stay here and start shooting, hold them off for 2 minutes and come after me as fast as you can, go straight down the hallway I will be waiting for you there. So we started firing, you have to hand it to the red shirts, they had disciple. We were just opening up on them like firing at the ducks in a carnival but they would fire back they just kept coming. Running over their own, jumping down the steps, using each other as shields, moving towards us anyway they could.

Pam and Julie were in the zone, Ben's death and the cold war that they had going between them that has turned into molten lava was helping them with their motivation. I was just watching the time, Einstein with his relativity theory, of space and time seems so boring until your life is on the line, it's only then when you notice how precious every second can be. Right now as there are hundreds and hundreds of men trying to kill us, I marvel at the shimmering lights in Julie's hair as it bounces.

The millions of years that was the last two minutes ends I grab the woman we start running down the narrow dim corridor. We have a good 10 to 15 second head start on the red shirts. But it didn't take us long to see the door and BOB waiting for us.

"Come on run"

BOB was yelling at us with that tone parents take when there cheering on the kids at the swim meets, love and exasperation. We fall into the room which is pitch black and I see BOB's back kind of move down on something and see the door slowly close and the little light of a hallway fades away and the yells of the red shirts fade away. I trip and I am lying on a cold floor in complete darkness, a darkness more complete than shutting my eyes.

Lights start to flicker and I see we were in a huge concrete tube and the door was a circler bank door, so thick you couldn't even hear our friends out there, but I knew they were trying everything they could. I got up and moved over to the door, memory is a funny thing, strange things go down paths of the mind and pull back things you thought lost.

As I moved to the door I felt my memoires searching, for something needing a clue, and then I saw the plaque on the door PS 91.

"My god." It was the ghost school

We walked, sometime in light and sometime in shadow, the walls are lined from floor to ceiling with shelves and endless supplies. Food, old, books, guns, knives on and on and on, like an ark for all the stuff of America it was all here.

GI Joe toys, black and white TV's, VCR's and car phones. Like the man who created this safe house couldn't decide what could be important and what could be trivial in the future so he just made sure everything was here. Hawaiian shirts and books on the Buda, orange soda and the Bible and on it went collecting dust for some future historian or archeologist to assign his own witty interpretation to the box of tampax discovered at the dig site.

We walk like zombies down a long incline and a huge garage door opens up and the wind and water hits our faces like a huge kiss from Mother Nature. I step over the lip of the door and just stood there breathing in the fresh air, joy, it's a word that hardly applies to anything in modern life, I felt joy, even before I saw the rather impressive arch of steel spanning the Hudson that is the George Washington bridge.

That is why we don't use joy in our vocabulary anymore, it's so fleeting, and so gossamer even as it fills your chest with love the world always works to destroy it. This time it was pushed out my body by the image of Pam pushing Julie to the ground face first. She pulled out blade she must have picked up from that long hallway of the debris if the 20th century.

She raised the blade over her head and totally committed to a dive into Julie chest, she looked like a world wrestler coming in for the smack down, only with a high-grade steel blade in her hands. BOB foot caught PAM in the stomach and knocked her over. Pam rolled and she and Julie got up together, Julie had pulled out a blade of her own and both woman where in that crouch that has served human kind for millions of years.

"Well Vic, here we are, you will have to chose, and only one can make it across the bridge with you."

"What?"

"Only couples are allowed across the bridge and three is not a couple, even I can't make that happen, the laws of math are really hard to break, physics is cake compared to them. So, you have to choose one to take with you and one to stay and die"

"I can't..."

Julie made the jump this time, well not really a jump it was a fake to her left side and when Pam moved back Julie went for her leg and got a good stab in.

"You know what that say, behind every mediocre man is a weak woman holding him back." Julie had been giving the opening of a life time her husband dead, the only thing standing in her way was the woman in front of her.

Pam was holding her leg and crying, but not from the knife pain, but a realization that Julie was right.

"Pam don't." She looked at me in the eyes and we both knew what I meant, I had made a choice after all.

Pam. God bless her, could always see a weakness and this time the weakness was her. She ran at Julie fast her knife right in front of her with a stiff arm; she knew exactly what Julie would do. Julie made a small step to her right and stabbed her right in the chest; combined with the Pam running it went right up into the hilt. They stood there looking at each other.

"You are strong on the outside, but to help him you're going to have to be strong on the inside. Time to step it up little big boobs."

With that my wife fell to the floor and I ran to her side, I felt nothing..

Death is silence a silence you never find in life, with our hearts pounding our blood moving, endless digestion and endless thoughts we never have that kind of silence. For

Pam, poor Pam, who was never at peace with herself, I saw in death the one thing she could never find in life. Peace. We just stayed there, the wind and mist washing over us; I knew she would have liked it here, the moss growing on the wet rocks.

Then we heard it again, the sounds of people, lot of them, it was the red shirts, climbing down the rocks to us. Some of them falling down on the rocks, other climbing on each other, screaming always screaming.

"Well, looks like the end of the road for me."

"What?" Julie and I said it at the same time.

"We won't make it to the bridge no matter how fast we run, so I'm going to have to buy you two a some time."

"No, we can make it."

"No we can't." Bob started walking to them, checking his guns along the way.

"Stop, please stop" Julie was screaming, pleading, begging but Bob wouldn't stop he was heading right to them, walking slowly.

Then he stopped

"Vic, I'm the start up band, the opening act, the closer is with you two, and so make sure you make it across the bridge." Julie was staring at him.

"Come on Julie you have to feel it, something different in you something alive. Just do me one favor, take your time naming the kid, I always hated the name Bob."

"What?"

But Bob didn't answer, he just kept walking to them and they started to converge on him. For a couple of seconds I saw him like the first time I saw him playing on his little video game, until the circle closed around him. Even half a block away we could hear it, that sound that must have been released into every sky on this planet, in every age that horrible sound of hunger and biting and grasping and clawing.

"No, No, No" Julie ran towards the mob but I had her arm and pulled the other way. Soon they would come for me, come for us and I was waiting welcoming the release, welcoming the freedom from the thing I had become. But they didn't come; they just stood there looking at us and the bridge.

The walk across the center of the GWB is eerie, all the cars are gone and there was a solider about every 10 paces. The bridge is long and the wind pretty much makes you death. I was holding Julie's hand the whole way and she was crying. We didn't know what was going to happen on the other side, but we had each other, love and a someone on the way, everything else is gravy.